"Cody is your son."

Everything in Lance's life shifted. "Why tell me now, Tamara? When you know it's going to change everything between us?"

"I don't know!" Tamara swallowed. "But please don't take him away from me."

A wave of emotion—something hot and jumbled and powerful—filled his throat. "I would never take him from you. But I'd like to get to know him."

Tamara's smile was grateful. "There's one more thing. Last night can't happen again. I like you too much to let myself fall in love with you."

For a moment Lance was seized with a vision of her, lying like a sleek cat, her face awash with the rosy flush of passion. If she had said anything else just then, he would have argued. But something in him ached as he reached out and touched her cheek. "You're right. I like you, too. Too much to do you wrong—and I would, eventually."

Dear Reader,

Those long days of summer sunshine are just around the corner—and Special Edition has six fabulous new books to start off the season right!

This month's THAT'S MY BABY! title is brought to you by the wonderful Janis Reams Hudson. *His Daughter's Laughter* tells the poignant tale of a widowed dad, his fragile little girl and the hope they rediscover when one extraordinary woman touches their lives.

June is the month of wedding bells—or in some cases, wedding blues. Be sure to check out the plight of a runaway bride who leaves one groom behind, only to discover another when she least expects it in *Cowboy's Lady*—the next installment in Victoria Pade's ongoing A RANCHING FAMILY miniseries. And there's more romance on the way with award-winning author Ruth Wind's *Marriage Material*— book one in THE LAST ROUNDUP, a new cross-line series with Intimate Moments about three brothers who travel the rocky road to love in a small Colorado town.

And speaking of turbulent journeys, in *Remember Me?* Jennifer Mikels tells a passionate love story about an amnesiac woman who falls for the handsome hero who rescues her from a raging rainstorm. Also in June, Shirley Larson presents *That Wild Stallion*—an emotional Western that's sure to tug your heartstrings.

Finally, *New York Times* bestselling author Ellen Tanner Marsh lives up to her reputation with *A Doctor in the House*, her second Silhouette title. It's all work and no play for this business executive until he meets his match in the form of one feisty Southern beauty in the Florida Keys!

I hope you enjoy all our summer stories this month!

Sincerely,

Tara Gavin
Senior Editor

Please address questions and book requests to:
Silhouette Reader Service
U.S.: 3010 Walden Ave., P.O. Box 1325, Buffalo, NY 14269
Canadian: P.O. Box 609, Fort Erie, Ont. L2A 5X3

RUTH WIND

MARRIAGE MATERIAL

Silhouette®

SPECIAL EDITION®

Published by Silhouette Books
America's Publisher of Contemporary Romance

For Krissie, known to all as Anne Stuart, to whom I owe more than I could ever repay. Lance is for you, Sister K. <wink>

 SILHOUETTE BOOKS

ISBN 0-373-24108-9

MARRIAGE MATERIAL

Copyright © 1997 by Barbara Samuel

This edition published by arrangement with Harlequin Books S.A.

® and TM are trademarks of Harlequin Books S.A., used under license. Trademarks indicated with ® are registered in the United States Patent and Trademark Office, the Canadian Trade Marks Office and in other countries.

Printed in U.S.A.

Books by Ruth Wind

Silhouette Special Edition

Strangers on a Train #555
Summer's Freedom #588
Light of Day #635
A Minute To Smile #742
Jezebel's Blues #785
Walk In Beauty #881
The Last Chance Ranch #977
Rainsinger #1031
*Marriage Material #1108

Intimate Moments

Breaking the Rules #587

*The Last Roundup

RUTH WIND

is the award-winning author of both contemporary and historical romance novels. She lives in the mountainous Southwest with her husband, two growing sons and many animals, in a hundred-year-old house the town blacksmith built. The only hobby she has had since she started writing is tending the ancient garden of irises, lilies and lavender beyond her office window, and she says she can think of no more satisfying way to spend a life than growing children, books and flowers.

Excerpt from the diary of
Louise Forrest...

Lance is coming home! Said he couldn't let Forrest Construction leave the family, not after everything his daddy poured into it.

Tonight I'm remembering all kinds of things about that boy of mine...thinking about that charming smile that gets him out of so much trouble, and the mischief always right there under the surface, glinting out of those blue eyes. Heaven knows I love all my boys, but I've sure missed Lance. He's just so pleased with everything all the time, as if life is one giant adventure and he never met a minute he didn't like. He loves all of it. Mornings and fishing and pretty women and loud music and even a good fight.

That makes him kind of wild, and impossible to hold, but it isn't as if he pretends to be anything but just what he is—a footloose rebel with a big appetite for life (and a heart of gold).

I'm just afraid that he won't ever settle down.

Speaking of that, I saw Tamara Jensen at the grocery store the other day, and I'd swear that little boy of hers is a Forrest, through and through. But neither Jake nor Tyler has claimed him, and now I'm thinking it's a lot more likely it was my Lance who sowed a few wild oats at some time or another. I wonder if Cody might be his...?

Wouldn't that be interesting?

Chapter One

Lance Forrest hit Red Creek, Colorado, much the same way as he always did—radio blaring so loud it seemed as if his car were floating on the sound. Rock and roll, naturally. Through the windows blew a light, dry mountain wind, combing playful fingers through his always too-long hair. He breathed the air deep, all the way to the bottom of his lungs, smelling the sharply evocative mix of sunlight and crushed pine needles on earth just faintly damp.

He'd been living in Houston, where the air weighed three hundred pounds per square inch, and nothing could have been finer than the sweet mountain air of home. He hung his elbow out the window, feeling a faint hint of September bite. The aspens, shaking their gold-coin leaves against a sky the color of a little girl's Easter ribbon, already showed autumn had arrived.

Red Creek wasn't much of a town. Barely three thousand people if you didn't count the tourists and skiers and the new crop of rich folks building half-million dollar "retreats" on enormous parcels of land buried in the trees. Lance didn't. Not many of them stayed year-round. Even fewer had the faintest clue what Colorado really meant.

As he reached the outskirts of town, he noticed a few changes—the grocery store had been revamped to look like any big-time supermarket. A brand-name pizza parlor camped next to the lone motel. Next to the old Rexall drugstore, where Lance had spent many hours over ice-cream sodas, a gourmet coffee shop and French bakery offered upscale breakfast goodies.

Not so bad. It would be unrealistic to expect the place to stay completely preserved year after year. Lance could live with a few changes. Cheerfully, he waved to everyone he saw, grinning at the double takes they did at his car.

His car. It was a beauty, all right. A 1965 Ford Fairlane, silver-gray, with white walls and an engine designed when gas was a quarter a gallon. It rumbled like a street rod as he ambled up Main Street, the engine purring even at seven thousand feet above sea level. It was his pride and joy, this car, fully restored down to the last detail.

His father would have loved it.

Glancing in the rearview mirror, Lance saw the black-and-white sheriff's car that had fallen in behind him. He grinned. Right on time. Sheriff Holloran never let him get past the Kwick Shop without a tail, and it hardly would have felt like a proper homecoming without the escort. Holloran no doubt hoped to catch him swigging from an open beer, but not even Lance was fool enough to drink and try to navigate the mountain passes over which he'd driven. He half wished he had one now, though, just to nettle Holloran. The old man must have missed Lance after so long a time—who else would give him so much to do?

At the traffic light by the courthouse, Lance lifted his green bottle of soda pop, and waved at the sheriff over his shoulder. Damn, it was good to be home.

Even if it was for a funeral.

Tamara Flynn wiped glasses desultorily and glanced at the clock. One more hour and she was free. She put the glass neatly in its place on the rubber matting behind the bar and turned to pick up another, trying to hide a yawn by lowering her head.

Not that anyone would notice. There were only a handful of customers at the Wild Moose Inn this early in the day. A pair of retirees had taken up permanent residence over a backgammon board in the booth in the corner. A closemouthed traveling salesman who drove through Red Creek on Mondays and Fridays on his way to and from Denver, nursed his single beer. A handful of construction workers, off for three days to mark the passing of old man Forrest—he'd dropped dead of a heart attack right at this bar, one hand on a whiskey, the other reaching for a waitress's behind—played pool in the back room.

Late afternoons were always like this—slow and lazy. Tamara used the time to prepare the bar for the late shift, stocking the cooler full of bottled beer, and making fresh gallons of Bloody Marys and margaritas for the crowd that would come in later for the buffalo steaks, venison stew and antelope burgers that had made the place famous for twenty-five years.

Tending bar in an eccentric mountain bar and restaurant wasn't everyone's idea of a great job, but for Tamara, it was perfect. It let her squeeze in a half schedule of accounting classes at the community college every morning before she arrived at eleven, and let her off in time to fix dinner for her son, Cody, and spend some time with him before he went to bed.

A lock of hair escaped the fat band she used to hold it back, and Tamara took a second to tuck the errant strand back in. She glanced at the salesman's beer. He nursed one for almost an hour, and never had a second, but habits might change. This one hadn't. The beer was still half-full.

The bell above the door rang, and Tamara glanced up without much interest. Long fingers of buttery light slanted through the big front window and door, skidding off varnished yellow pine walls. The man in the doorway stood there silhouetted against that gold, as if allowing his eyes to adjust. For a single, fanciful moment, Tamara thought he looked as if he wore a halo.

There was a scrape of a chair toward the back, and Tamara glanced in that direction automatically. Only then did she become aware that the room had gone quiet. The knot of construction workers had come forward to stand in a ragged line in the archway to the back room, their attention focused on the new customer.

She looked back at the man with a frown, alert for trouble. He moved into the room with a marked lack of concern, as if he didn't see the burly group eyeing him.

His lazy stroll took him from the shadows into the flat square of sunshine spilling over the flat pine dance floor, and Tamara, almost without realizing it, caught her breath.

The dark gold hair was windblown and untidy and too long, but it caught the light in sinful, banded streaks. His face was sun lined and high planed. His eyes twinkled, and the lips almost smiled, as if he had a secret. There was cockiness in that expression, the kind of brash confidence some men seemed to own from birth.

Her gaze traveled downward, over his body. All man, one-hundred-percent American made: broad shouldered, with solid biceps and the hardy sort of forearms that came from swinging tools; lean hips and long legs, slightly bowed.

Against her will, Tamara found a half grin of her own forming. If he wasn't a man without a care in the world, he sure gave a good imitation.

What she wouldn't give to have that feeling again!

The dancing eyes fixed without worry on the burly line of men at the back room. "Hi, boys," he drawled.

Not one of them replied. Tamara thought of the television commercials, when a stranger came into a run-down, hot place and opened a beer, and the whole room filled with a snowstorm. That was the kind of wary, intense attention these men gave the newcomer, and he bore it with the same singular lack of concern.

He dropped onto a barstool, shoved untidy, windblown hair from his face and smiled. "I'll have a beer, sugar."

The endearment shouldn't have been a surprise. It went along with everything else. "What kind of beer?" she said, calmly meeting his eyes. Men knew the rules. If a woman wasn't swayed by pretty little gestures or outrageous flirting, they moved on fast enough.

The dancing in his eyes—dark blue—increased. "Cold one," he said.

Tamara sighed. Why did men always think that was so clever? Contrarily, she opened the cooler and pulled out the most expensive import. "Glass?"

"Just like that will be fine."

Even the most cynical of women would have had a hard time resisting that relentlessly good-natured almost-smile. Tamara looked away, trying to find something to do with herself. This was the hardest part of the job for her—when someone sat down at midbar and showed every sign of wanting to talk. She wasn't a chitchat sort of person.

"What's your name, darlin'?" he asked.

She plucked a snowy white bar towel off the sink and wiped the necks of the liquor bottles in the well. If she told him, maybe he'd stop the annoying endearments. "Tamara."

"Tamara, huh?" He took a sip of the expensive brew straight from the bottle, and inclined his head. "That can't be right."

"I'm afraid it is."

"Anyone call you Tammy?"

She lifted her brows. "Not if they wanted to live to tell about it."

He grinned widely, and Tamara saw against her will that there was an honest-to-God dimple deep in the left cheek. "Good," he said. "I used to know a real mean Tammy. She put pig piss in my thermos once."

Even the taciturn salesman looked up at that.

"That's disgusting," she said.

"Yep, it was. Luckily, my brother found out about it before I actually drank it."

Warning herself that it was a mistake, Tamara smiled.

"That's better," he said. "Always consider the day a success if I can make a pretty lady smile."

Tamara shook her head. "If you talked to Tammy like this, you deserved the thermos trick."

He chuckled. "I didn't say I didn't deserve it." He inclined his head. "You know, you make me think of..." The glinting eyes narrowed. "A cat I used to have. Big calico, with green eyes, just like yours."

She rolled her eyes, this time, not even bothering to hide it. "Mister, that's an old line."

"No way!" he protested, but the laughing eyes betrayed him.

Honestly, she felt a real laugh almost break the surface over that. It was impossible to mind being hustled when it was so blatantly offered as exactly that. She put a hand on her hip. "You've yet to come up with a single original line, as a matter of fact."

He looked at the salesman. "Is she always this tough?"

The salesman who'd never uttered more than the required words to get his beer now rubbed his chin. "No nonsense, more like."

"Goes with the territory," Tamara said in her defense.

The golden man let go of a low chuckle. Tamara

found her eyes on his mouth, on the white teeth and long brown throat. A faint, almost forgotten sensation of awareness moved in her.

"Well, it gives you a nice aura of mystery," he said. His voice was not deep or rough, as might have suited him, but a pleasant tenor that was surprisingly easy to listen to. "And you know men—we like women who have a few mysteries."

"Well," she countered, "you know women. We like men with a little bit of sense."

Again, he let go of a delighted laugh. "One of the great conundrums of life, don't you think?"

Tamara was surprised at his use of the word—it didn't strike her as part of the ordinary vocabulary of the kind of man he seemed to be. The assumption that he would be stupid stung her conscience for a moment and she smiled. "I guess it is."

An odd stir in the atmosphere of the bar made her nerves prickle. Tamara looked up, alert and frowning. She'd tended bar long enough to recognize that kind of warning—and her instincts were right.

The restless construction workers from the back room had drifted out, one or two at a time, until they were spread throughout the room. One stood at the pass-out bar, two by the front door, another dead center of the room. The last, a burly, dark-haired finisher named Gus, with a beer gut straining the front of his old white T-shirt, swaggered over to stand beside the man at the bar.

Trouble. Damn.

Tamara pushed away from the bar and backed up slowly toward the door that led to the empty restaurant.

"Tamara," said the sun-gilded man at the bar, reaching into his pocket for money as if Gus and the others were invisible, "I think I'm ready for another beer."

He stood up, took some bills out of the front pocket of his jeans and sat back down. Tamara turned, ready to run for the other room. He might be stupid enough not to recognize the hatred bristling through the room, but she didn't intend to be in the middle of a fight when it broke out.

The construction worker who'd been at the pass-out bar stepped back three paces, blocking Tamara's way to the restaurant.

She narrowed her eyes and thought of the phone. As if he read her mind, he backed up another foot and leaned his considerable shoulders against the receiver. He gave her an apologetic glance. "Sorry, honey. Old Gus has been waiting for this a long time. That man stole his girl."

Gus bellied up to the man at the bar now. "Well, well, well," he said with false joviality. "Lance Forrest. 'Bout time you brought yourself back here."

The name hit Tamara hard. She narrowed her eyes. Lance Forrest, the legendary wild man of Red Creek, by all accounts a hell-raiser that put even his father to shame. Her heart speeded up.

She'd been on duty the night Olan Forrest had dropped dead of a heart attack. She'd been on duty a hundred nights before that when she had to call him a cab, or have a bouncer toss him out, or knock his wandering hands aside when she served him.

Hard to believe this gorgeous creature, who seemed

made of sunlight, could be in anyway related to that bad-tempered womanizer.

It also explained a lot. Tamara felt her mouth go tight. Lance Forrest. It was about time. He wasn't exactly what she'd expected after all these years, but that freewheeling nature would fit neatly into her plans.

Revenge. That was what she wanted. And she'd waited four long years for this chance.

But at the moment, there were more important problems to consider. Like how to get out of here before the whole place turned into a melee.

Tamara glanced at the salesman. He caught her eye steadily, and she put as much pleading as she could into the glance. He stood up and backed away. No one paid him any attention.

Lance looked up, a lock of that bright hair falling over his eye. There wasn't an iota of fear his face, she noted with a little panic. Was he that stupid?

"Hey, Gus," he drawled, and Tamara would have sworn there was a twinkle in those blue eyes.

Tamara couldn't stand it. "Don't you dare have a fight in my bar," she said. "Not if you ever want to drink here again."

Gus looked at her. "Nothing personal, Tamara," he said regretfully. Fast as lightning, he turned and threw a punch. Lance ducked, but not quite fast enough. A fist caught him across the eye.

"Stop it!" Tamara shouted.

Lance came up swinging, barreling into Gus with a grunt, and driving him backward into the wall. Two framed pictures of trout crashed to the floor. From the back room came the sound of the jukebox, kicking into a rowdy, loud country-western song.

It covered the noise of the fight. It was only Gus and Lance, roaring and tumbling over the space of the dance floor, knocking chairs and tables askew. The rest of the construction workers simply stood sentry at various doors and made sure no one else jumped in.

It happened so fast there was no time to react in the first few seconds, but as the two men spun around the room like a couple of brawlers in an old-time saloon, knocking things down, crushing furniture, Tamara lost her temper.

"Stop it!" she yelled again, and tried to round the bar, shoving at the man who blocked her way with a furious hand. "They're trashing the place!" she cried. "Break it up."

He didn't move. Tamara backed away, and heard another crash. She whirled and saw a table go over, spilling salt and pepper. A tall jar of sugar crashed to the floor. She stared at the mess blankly for a second, thinking of how much work she'd have to do when these idiots quit their wrestling. Dinner would be late again, and she had an accounting test in the morning to study for.

Without a second thought, she jumped on to the bar, and then to the floor, vaguely planning to head for the door—or at least the pay phone near the rest rooms.

She dodged the guy closest by her, ducking down low to avoid him, and slipped out of his reach. Feeling victorious, she straightened to run for the door—

—and a fist came from nowhere and slammed into her face. The force of the punch landed right below her eye. Stunned, Tamara tumbled backward, feeling hands catch her as she fell.

Chapter Two

"Damn it, Gus," Lance said, eyeing the pretty bartender, who now was sprawled on the floor, her hand cradled to her face. "Now look what you've done!"

Lance was trying to get out of this without hurting the big dumb dog, but the bartender was the last straw. Lance turned, doubled back and landed an elbow to Gus's midsection. The air whooshed from him. Lance called up his famous left to the face—you didn't brawl with an older brother for a decade without learning a few tricks—and a right to the gut. Gus went down.

His friends moved forward. "Don't," Lance said, wiping his mouth. A little blood, but not bad. He licked it experimentally, breathing hard from exertion. "One of y'all needs to go get the manager right now, or clear your butts outta here before the cops come. No point in all of us going to jail tonight."

They weren't as dumb as Gus, and most of them were likely in deep trouble with their wives for drinking up their paychecks as it was. They disappeared, leaving Gus grunting in the middle of the floor.

The woman sat on the floor by the barstool, blinking, her hand covering the place on her face where Gus had punched her. Lance knelt. "You all right?"

The bewilderment hadn't worn off yet. She blinked those great big cat-green eyes at him as if she didn't speak his language.

He reached out, and she drew back, wincing, as if she would be hit again. He paused. "I just want to see if you're hurt, okay?"

Still she stared at him without comprehension. He moved slowly, reaching for her hand, which she held protectively over her cheek. It was a long-fingered, slim hand. Elegant in shape, but work worn. He carefully lifted her fingers from her face. "I'm just going to look at it, honey."

She lowered her eyes, turning her face away. Lance caught her chin and lifted it toward the light. A blazing red mark showed across the cheekbone. By morning, it would be a big, ugly bruise, and she'd have a shiner like a brawler.

He grimaced. "I know that hurt." A taste of blood struck his tongue, and he wiped his cut lip quickly. He took her hand and pulled her up. "Let's get some ice on it right now."

She let herself be led to the end of the bar. "You're bleeding," she said as he grabbed a bar towel.

"It won't kill me." He filled the bar towel full of ice and twisted the ends, then lifted it to her face.

"That really hurt," she said.

It still hadn't sunk in. Lance wanted to get out of there before it did—she struck him as a woman who might be dangerous if her temper were engaged.

But a part of him was reluctant to leave just yet. Up close she smelled faintly of margaritas and the clean sweat of a woman's hard work, but there were lingering notes of some kind of light, flowery perfume. Not too sweet—maybe lavender. His mother grew banks of it along the back porch and he'd always liked the scent of it on an evening wind.

"You want to sit down?" he asked.

"For a minute."

He pushed her onto the stool behind the bar, and quickly poured a glass of water that he put beside her. "I'm gonna have to get out of here before the sheriff comes to haul me to jail. My mother's gonna kill me as it is."

"Your mother?" she echoed. "Men like you don't have mothers."

"Now, see, that's where you're wrong." A stab through his ribs straightened him suddenly. He grunted, putting a hand on the place where Gus's beefy fist had landed all too solidly. "We do. They just despair of ever civilizing us."

Her smile bloomed then, one more time. The pink lips curled, slowly, and a light wash of color touched her pale cheeks. Her entire face was transformed from the slightly defensive hard look of bartenders who had to deal with men like him day in and day out, and became something else. Something sweet he hadn't even been aware of missing.

"You're really pretty, you know it?" he said, and impulsively touched her unmarked cheek.

She only gazed at him. Still stunned.

Sirens sounded distantly and Lance looked over his shoulder. "That's my cue." From the pocket of his jeans, he took a roll of bills and peeled off several, which he put on the bar next to her glass of water. "Give that to Allen and tell him I'm sorry. Take care now." He winked. "I'll be back."

As he leapt into his car, hearing the sirens come closer, he remembered he'd forgotten to leave a tip.

Louise Forrest was in her element. As weary as she was from attending to what seemed like hundreds of details for her husband's burial, she felt perfectly calm as she lifted the lid on a bubbling pot of black-eyed peas. The bacon-scented steam made her mouth water. She smiled. The peas were for her youngest son, Tyler, who could never get enough of the Southern treat she'd brought with her as a seventeen-year-old Texas bride.

In the oven was a ham baked with pineapple, for Jake, her oldest. And in a big bowl in the fridge was the fruit salad made with whipped cream that Lance loved.

Her boys. It was hard to believe they'd all be home, together. She literally couldn't remember the last time that had happened.

Mary, her housekeeper, bustled into the kitchen. "Louise Forrest, what are you doing? You can't keep going like this! You'll collapse."

"Don't be silly. Cooking relaxes me."

"It isn't natural for a new widow to be so calm." Mary frowned. "I'm worried about you."

Louise turned. "I wish you'd stop insisting I should

take to my bed.'' She lowered her voice, for Jake and Tyler sat in the other room, watching the television news.''I'll mourn my husband in my own way, in my own time.''

Mary sighed loudly, but tied an apron around her waist and made preparations for setting the table.

Louise frowned. Mary knew as well as anyone that Olan had barely shown his face within these walls for almost five years. She could count on one hand the number of times he'd actually slept here in that time. Louise had gone back to college and Olan, in a snit, took a mistress.

She would mourn him no more and no less than she'd mourn any old, but distant acquaintance. She wished it could be more, but the marriage had been hollow for a very long time.

The rumble of a big car engine sounded in the yard behind the house. Louise wiped her hands, hurried to the window and spied Lance getting out of a sixties Ford, lovingly restored. Her heart pinched—poor Lance. Of all of them, he'd mourn his father most sincerely. A part of her was glad that Olan would have someone to regret his passing, even if he'd done his best to drive this child away.

It was only as Lance slammed the door and turned toward the house that she realized he'd been fighting. Her mouth tightened. He looked like a tomcat that had just crawled out of the bushes, his beautiful hair tangled, his clothes disheveled, his mouth bleeding. There was something white wrapped around his knuckles.

''Been at it again, hasn't he?'' said Mary, behind her.

"I reckon." Nonetheless, Louise smiled. Her boys were home.

Lance climbed the back steps carefully, a stabbing pain in his ribs. He hoped none of them was broken. On the next to the top step, he remembered the presents he'd brought for his mother, and limped back down to retrieve them. Carrying a grocery store bouquet of red carnations laced with baby's breath—her favorite—and a box of chocolate-covered cherries, he climbed back up the steps.

His nephew Curtis, small and blond and round at three, was the first to greet him. The boy blasted through the back screen door, leaving it to slam behind. "Uncle Lanth!" he cried, and let go of the chortle peculiar to little kids, an unthrottled joy that always struck right to the bottom of Lance's heart.

Lance knelt and caught Curtis by the legs. "Boy," he grunted—gasping at the sharp stab in his right side, "you're getting too big to carry! Where's your grandma and your dad?"

"Inthide." His big blue eyes went wide and he folded his little hands solemnly. "Grandpa's in heaven."

Not likely, Lance thought, but he kissed Curtis. "I know, slugger."

Curtis gingerly touched Lance's cut lip. "You have an owie? Grandma gots Band-Aids. G.I. Joe."

Lance laughed and nuzzled his face into Curtis's chest. "I missed the hell out of you, boy."

They went inside together, into the kitchen that was now crowded with the family waiting for the last of their fold. Lance's mother hugged him first, smelling of her trademark Chanel perfume. She exclaimed over the flowers and tsked happily over the box of chocolates. "You know I don't need this!" she protested, gesturing at her ample hips.

Then she slapped his arm. "You couldn't wait three days to have a fight, huh?" she said with a frown, peering at his lip.

"I swear, Mama, I didn't start it."

"Sure, sure," said Tyler, his younger brother, from the doorway. His *little* brother, who now stood taller than any of them.

Lance frowned. "Hell, man, you going mountain man on us?" Ty's pale blond hair was long, caught back in a ponytail, and there was a shadow of light beard on his jaw. "Don't be trying to grow a beard and make a fool of yourself, now," he said, and hugged him, pleased when a smile broke Ty's all-too-serious expression.

The last to give him a welcome was Jake, as dark as his brothers were fair, his hair months past the military cut he'd sported for almost twenty years. "Hope the other guy looks worse," Jake said ironically.

Lance thought of the bartender with a twinge of guilt. She was the only real victim in the whole thing. "He went down first, anyway."

"Go get cleaned up," Louise said. "Supper is almost ready and I don't want to be waiting on you."

Impulsively, Lance bent and kissed her cheek. "Yes, ma'am," he said. "Come on, Curtis, you can help carry my suitcase in."

"Okay!" In little cowboy boots, Curtis clunked after him.

Home, Lance thought, breathing deeply of the gathering evening that fell in the backyard. The sun lingered in a pale yellow haze behind the jagged mountains towering around the house, and a few birds clung to the pines, their whistles a wistful sound in the air that suddenly had a deep bite to it.

Home. Thank God.

Tamara had the worst headache in the history of the world, and Cody wasn't doing much to help. She'd managed to get him fed—applesauce with macaroni and cheese out of a box—and into the bathtub. Now she sat on the closed toilet in her little house, supervising, thinking with exhaustion of the test she yet had to study for. Accounting—her worst subject. She hated math.

"Look, Mommy!" Cody cried, pointing to the circle he'd drawn on his taut four-year-old tummy with a blue soap crayon.

"Beautiful," she said with a nod. "Come on, kidlet, hurry up. I need to wash your hair."

"No," Cody protested, covering his blond curls with his hands. "I hate that."

"I got new shampoo. It won't hurt if you get some in your eyes." Tamara picked up the bottle of baby shampoo to show him. On Saturday, she'd had to use some of her own shampoo. Cody had gotten into one of his silly moods while the shampoo was in his hair, and it had burned his eyes. "See?" She pointed to the label. "That says it won't hurt."

The doorbell rang. Tamara frowned in surprise. No one ever came to see her. She was, frankly, too busy to have time to indulge the nurturing friendships required. "Don't move," she said to Cody.

She walked to the doorway of the bathroom, her eyes on Cody, and called, "Who is it?"

"It's me," came a door-deadened voice. "Lance Forrest. I was in the fight at the bar this afternoon."

Lance Forrest. For a minute she bit her lip. "What do you want?"

"Just to make sure you're okay."

Even through the door, she liked the sound of his voice. Warm and not too dark, with a hint of a country drawl. Something unidentified moved through her. Annoying her.

"I have a present for you," he called when she didn't answer.

She rolled her eyes. "Give it to your mother." From the corner of her eye, she saw Cody put the soap in his mouth. "Cody, quit that!"

He made a face and tried to wipe away the blue soap on his lips.

"I already gave my mama a present," Lance said. "Come on, Tamara. I feel bad."

Cody bent his face toward the water. Tamara called out, "Oh, come on in!" and made a dash for the tub. "Let me help you, honey." She fished a washcloth from the water and wiped away the blue soap. "There."

She heard the front door open, and thought immediately of her clothes. An old, oversize T-shirt and a pair of sweats that had seen better days. She couldn't remember the last time she'd brushed her hair. No help for it now.

"In the bathroom, straight ahead," she called.

Defensively, she smoothed her shirtfront and pushed

a lock of hair out of her face. She had to be crazy, even letting him in.

"Hi," he said, coming around the corner. He'd changed clothes since this afternoon, and wore a pair of button-fly jeans. He'd evidently worn them since time began, for the color was bleached nearly white, and the fit was practically indecent. The sinfully streaked hair glinted as brightly in the bathroom light as it had in the sunshine this afternoon, but now it had been brushed neatly, and his jaw was cleanly shaved. His shoulders seemed to fill the doorway.

For one instant, a moment filled with pure, unadulterated longing, Tamara wished she'd never heard his name. Then she'd be free to explore the promise that shimmered around him like an almost inaudible song.

But she *had* heard his name. All too often. And had learned to hate it.

From the bathtub, Cody chirped a cheery "Hi!"

Lance gave the boy a crooked smile. "Howdy!"

A queer nervousness rolled in Tamara's stomach, unexpected and worrisome. She looked at Cody. Blond and blue-eyed, his face was baby round, but would one day have the same carved planes as his father. His father, who was proving much harder to hate in person than in her imagination. Tamara hardened her resolve. For her cousin Valerie and the son she'd borne, Tamara could face the devil himself.

She looked at Lance. "That's Cody," she said. Would he see anything of himself in the boy? Probably not. You didn't see what you didn't expect. There were millions of blond, blue-eyed boys in the world.

"Hey, Cody. I like those tattoos."

Cody lifted an arm and flexed his thin muscle, mak-

ing the white Power Ranger figure move his legs.
"Lookit what he does."

"Cool." Lance hadn't moved from the threshold of
the door, and now half lifted a small grocery bag in
Tamara's direction. "Brought you something."

There was no amusement in his face now, no secret
twinkle in the blue eyes. He looked...worn. Even so,
it was the most singularly compelling face she'd ever
seen. Strong bones, a beautifully shaped nose, the
bright, bright blue eyes made even brighter by the
depth of his tan.

"I guess I caught you at a bad time," he said, and
licked his swollen lower lip.

"No worse than any other," Tamara said. "What
do you want?"

"Who are you?" Cody asked.

"My name is Lance."

"Mr. Forrest," Tamara corrected.

Lance nodded. "Right. Mr. Forrest."

"Do you live in the forest?" Cody asked, and
laughed at his joke.

"Matter of fact, I do." The twinkle leapt back to
life in his eyes, and Tamara felt a strange sense of
relief. "About a million trees all around."

"Wow ."

Before the delay cost her any more time than necessary, Tamara spoke up. "I have to get him to bed.
What exactly do you want?"

Lance sobered once more, and stepped forward to
give her the bag he carried. "A steak," he said with
a lift of one shoulder. "First you put it on your eye,
then you eat it, and you'll feel a lot better by morning."

She took the bag and peeked inside. A thick, beautiful T-bone. In spite of herself, she felt a stab of hunger. Macaroni and cheese worked for Cody, but every so often, it would be nice to eat like an adult.

Nonetheless, she held it out to him. "Thanks, but no thanks."

"Oh, come on, what'll it hurt?"

She glanced at Cody, who listened intently. "Take the steak for a second, will you?" She picked up a towel. "Let me get this child out of the tub."

"I'll help you."

"That isn't—" she began, but Cody had already stood up, shivering, and Lance wrapped the boy in a towel. He held Cody close, pretending to shiver, and Tamara's protest died in her throat.

She wasn't truly prepared to see the resemblance between them, but even with the softness of toddlerhood still on him, Cody was a carbon copy of his father. A sudden and unexpected fear stabbed her stomach. What if Lance turned around right now and looked in the mirror? Would he see what was so plain to Tamara?

But he didn't turn. With typical little-boy trust, Cody yawned and put his head on Lance's shoulder. Lance rubbed a big tanned hand over the little back, as naturally as he'd swung his fists in the bar.

The picture pierced her. Lance wasn't supposed to be gentle—that much she knew. To hide her expression, she turned away, reaching to pull the plug from the drain. "If you put him down, he can go get dressed."

"All by himself?" Lance said in an admiring tone. "Man, you're really a big kid, aren't you?" He set the boy on his feet and straightened, watching as Cody pitter-pattered from the bathroom, towel clutched around him.

Tamara picked up the bag and held it out firmly. "Take your steak and all your little charming tricks and leave, please."

He didn't move. For a minute, he only looked at her, his eyes sober. "You don't like me, do you?"

"I don't know you."

"First impressions can be misleading. I don't have a fight every time I go into a bar."

She set the grocery bag on the edge of the sink beside him and crossed her arms. "I don't want to be rude, but I have a headache, and a test to study for, and I don't have time for all this."

He nodded, and she tried not to notice the way the light broke in bright gold bands in his hair, like threads of fool's gold in iron pyrite. "All right," he said. "Keep the steak. It really will help."

"No. Take it with you."

He looked at her, puzzlement in his blue eyes. "I'm trying to make amends here. Help me out a little, huh?"

"I don't want your amends, thank you. I don't want anything from you. I just want you to leave."

For a long, quiet minute, he simply looked at her. Tamara felt a fluttering disturbance in those private, untouched parts of her body she'd thought might have finally got the message by now.

Obviously not.

Pinned in the soberness of his formerly twinkling eyes, she wished she could accept everything he offered. Not just the steak. Much more—the promise of pleasure and laughter, the promise of a few hours unburdened with the worries that ate up her days. Men like this made an art form of sex—the kind of sex that made you forget everything and just live.

An unwelcome prickle of awareness moved on her shoulders, down her back. It had been so long....

The trouble was, a few pleasurable hours was the sum total of *all* he offered, and her life wasn't that simple. Not anymore. She crossed her arms. "Please, just go."

"I am sorry you got hurt, Tamara," he said. "Maybe I'll see you around town."

She said nothing. If she gave him nothing to embroider upon, he'd have to leave sooner or later.

At last, he did just that—turned away from her and ambled toward the bathroom door, then paused with his hand on the threshold. "See you around," he said again.

And gave her the most wicked, charming grin she'd ever seen—replete with seductive dimples and twinkling eyes and a teasing promise of seduction that stole her breath. Before she could react, he was out the front door, closing it quietly behind him.

She stood in the middle of the bathroom, arms crossed, and shook her head in wonder as she remembered the steak on the sink. That rat—he'd known exactly what he was doing.

Well, he could grin and wink and flash dimples for a year and a day. It wouldn't do him any good with Tamara. She had a real life to think about.

She got Cody tucked in, and heard his prayers. As he lay there on his pillow, printed with cartoon figures,

Tamara reminded herself it was all worth it. For Cody, she could do anything.

Her headache trebled when she opened her accounting book. Dry figures lay dully against the page, and she took a breath, fighting the deep resistance she felt. As she had told herself a hundred times, bookkeeping and accounting were good jobs, with benefits. Later, after they were on their feet, maybe she could finish her English degree.

Resolutely, she took out her notes and began crosschecking herself. The page didn't disappear, as it always had when she studied history and languages and literature, but she could do it.

She had to.

Chapter Three

An hour into her studies, Tamara rested her head on her arm. Just for a minute. Just to clear her eyes. Maybe ease the headache pounding through her temples.

She fell asleep. And dreamed she was at college again. She and Eric walked one of the avenues on campus, beneath trees shedding leaves in red and brown and yellow, their varied shapes dotting the withering lawn and floating atop the green water of the pond. The air was crisp and full of excitement. She and Eric debated the place of poets in the scope of history, swinging their hands between them.

Tamara jolted awake suddenly, yanked into her tiny kitchen in Red Creek by the sound of a tomcat in the garbage cans outside. She blinked slowly, an ache in her chest.

Four years, and she still dreamed about it all the time. Four years, and she had not come to terms with the fact that she would never be that free, excited girl again, with a future filled with intellectual pursuits, in the company of people who didn't think she was odd for enjoying French films or preferring to read rather than go to the rodeo.

At the university, for the first time in her life she'd found people to talk with about the things she loved. Music and books and history, a world of ideas and dreams and visions that most people around Red Creek found impractical at the very least.

She missed it desperately.

Wearily she closed the book and turned off the overhead light, making her way to the bathroom. She was almost too tired to shower, but if she left it till morning, she would be more rushed than she could stand. She stripped off her clothes and turned on the shower to let steam heat the small room.

In the mirror, she caught sight of her face. She leaned forward, gingerly touching the black eye. Her entire lid was purple, a garish contrast to her green iris. It added an impression of too many years on her youngish face, like the tightness around her mouth, the circles ringing her eyes. With a frown, she tugged out the braid and worked her fingers through the dark mass of her hair. Better. She didn't look so old and worn with it down.

She rubbed a circle in the misting mirror, looking for the girl she'd been only a few short years ago. Was her life over at twenty-five? Sometimes it felt like it.

The mirror swallowed her image once more. Tamara fixed the temperature of the water and stepped into the shower. The heated spray felt glorious on her tired neck and she sighed aloud, ducking her head to let the water pound down on the tight muscles. What a day.

A wavery picture of Lance Forrest floated before her closed eyes, then solidified. That bright hair. The twinkle in his eyes. The aura of zesty good humor that surrounded him. He made her think of Loki, the Norse god of mischief.

He wasn't at all what she had expected all these years.

Tamara's cousin Valerie had generally liked dark men—brooding, ruthless types who took what they wanted and strode through life without giving a second thought to the people around them. Bad boys. Jocks. Businessmen. Never the kind of man Tamara found attractive.

She should have realized, looking at Lance's brother Tyler, that Lance would not be the dark brooding man in her imagination, that vague image toward whom she had directed all her frustration and hatred all these years. If not for Lance Forrest, she had told herself over and over, she would be happily teaching in a university somewhere, working on her doctorate.

Instead, she was stuck in Red Creek, eating macaroni and cheese, studying accounting so she could eventually pay doctor bills, taking care of a child she adored and wanted, but wasn't even her own.

It was Valerie who had given birth to Cody.

Tamara and Valerie's mothers had come to Red Creek together, to make a new life for themselves far from their poverty-stricken Arkansas roots. To some degree, they had succeeded, but the sisters had very different ideas of what marked success and when Tamara was eight, they had a fight. They never spoke again.

But Valerie and Tamara managed to sneak around to see each other, anyway. Six years younger than her dazzling cousin, Tamara had worshiped the ground Valerie walked upon, and lived for the stories of romance and love Valerie spun.

When Valerie was in high school, she fell in love with Lance Forrest, and the pair were an item for their last two years there. Valerie had even shown Tamara the ring Lance had given her as a promise ring. It was a striking tigereye—he'd said diamonds were too common for a girl like Valerie.

But at the end of senior year, Lance had left Valerie and gone off to college. He never came back; instead he went to work for a Houston construction firm. Occasionally Valerie caught word here and there of what he was doing, but she never saw him when he came to town.

Finally, she gave up and married another man, and just as quickly divorced him. Tamara knew it was because Valerie had never quite gotten over her first love. It struck her young heart as deeply romantic—and tragic.

After her own high school graduation Tamara went to college at the University of Colorado at Denver. There she met Eric Marks, a philosophy major. By her sophomore year, they shared a small apartment and had planned a future in which they both taught at the same university. When Tamara's mother died at the start of her junior year, Tamara suffered a setback, but with Eric's support, managed to stay in school.

That Christmas, the first Christmas without her mother, Tamara received a letter from Valerie, telling her Lance Forrest had come home, and their love affair had been rekindled. Tamara worried, but Valerie sounded so happy, she tried to put aside her reservations.

But she'd been right to worry. After a brief—and by Valerie's accounts—torrid affair, Lance blew out of town just as quickly as he'd come in.

Leaving Valerie pregnant.

It had been the beginning of the end. By the time Spring Break rolled around, Tamara was worried enough about the wild ravings of Valerie's letters to go home and check on her. Valerie had always been a little unstable, prone to wild swings of emotion, but it had increased tenfold with pregnancy. Valerie had no one else—her own mother had gone back to Arkansas, washing her hands of her daughter.

Spring Break stretched to two weeks, then three. Eric made frantic, and increasingly irritated phone calls to Red Creek, urging Tamara to get back to school, but Tamara knew she couldn't live with herself if anything happened to her cousin.

Despite Tamara's efforts to get Valerie counseling, three months after Cody was born, Valerie drove herself off a high mountain road. It was ruled an accident, but Tamara knew better. When September came—the start of what should have been her senior year—Tamara was the adoptive mother of a baby son. Eric, disgusted with what he called her "provincial values," deserted her.

Tamara had stayed in Red Creek.

* * *

With a jolt, Tamara realized she'd been standing under the water for a long time. Her neck was still stiff, but better. She picked up the shampoo bottle—an expensive salon brand that was one of her few luxuries. Squeezing a tiny dot out in her palm, she began to wash her hair.

Now, she faced a moral dilemma. After almost four years of blaming Lance for everything, Tamara discovered he wasn't some dark evil man who'd stolen Valerie's virtue and deserted her. Not at all. He was what they would have called a rake in the old days, an unapologetic good-time Charlie who had no intention of ever settling down, but loved all the women he met along the way.

Which put Tamara's long-nursed plans of revenge in a new perspective. In the first place, she didn't quite know what sort of revenge she had meant to take. Her fantasies of making Lance pay had always been rather vague. She supposed she'd imagined making him fall in love with her, then breaking his heart, as he'd broken Valerie's.

The reality of his compelling physical presence made that seem a little absurd.

Valerie had planned to use Cody to get her revenge. In her more rational moments, Valerie had continually talked about it, her sapphire eyes cold and glittery. She planned to milk Lance Forrest of his money, using his own blood.

Tamara wouldn't do that. Cody was too precious to be used. Period.

So what possible revenge could there be? She had no money or power. Lance wasn't the kind of man who usually noticed her, so the seduction and broken heart angle were out. It was embarrassing that she'd even believed she might have a chance.

But then a vision of his wicked, promising grin flashed over her imagination.

What would it be like? Seducing him? Touching his golden skin, his sun-kissed hair, kissing his sensual mouth?

She shivered. *Don't even think about it.*

There was another angle she did have to think about. Cody.

Should Lance know about his child? Did he have any rights to a child he didn't even know existed?

No. Given his ways, he probably had dozens of children scattered around. One more wouldn't make any difference.

Wearily, she rinsed shampoo out of her eyes, then blinking, looked for the soap. The bar she used was over on the sink. Cody's crayon sat in the soap dish, and she picked it up with a giggle. What the heck.

She drew blue lines on her tummy, as he had. And down her arms, and her legs, feeling like a wild Scot. Remembering a movie she'd seen, she drew a line down the middle of her face, and rubbed blue crayon over the left side, and left it like that while she conditioned her hair. She wondered vaguely what battle she was preparing herself for.

But she knew. As her hands moved on her body, she remembered Lance Forrest's big masculine hands, with their square, strong fingers. Her nerves tingled at the thought, tingled in her stomach and her knees and along the back of her neck. Tingled in anticipation.

She was preparing for a battle with herself. With

her need to be touched like a woman. She ached to be stroked and pleasured, to be held and tended. It had been such a very long time.

And in that single moment, she knew she was going to do it. She was going to let Lance Forrest pursue her, keeping herself just out of his reach until he was in her clutches.

Then she would walk away, as he had walked away, leaving three broken lives behind him. For Valerie, for Cody and most of all, for her own broken dreams, she would do it. She would seduce Lance Forrest.

The morning of the funeral, Lance laid out his black suit, an Italian number a woman in Houston had picked out for him. He dressed carefully. Snowy shirt, silk socks, his good shoes. Before dawn broke, he got in his Fairlane, and went to the funeral home to say his goodbyes privately.

It was what people did, wasn't it? But the minute he stepped inside, Lance knew it was the wrong thing for him. The wrong way for him to bid farewell to his father. He shook his head at the funeral director and left.

He drove to a lake a few miles from town. And there in the outdoor stillness of morning, Lance felt his father. Here had Lance stood with his old man, learning to fish. Here had his father told him everything he deemed important. Here would Olan Forrest linger.

Lance put his head down. He wanted to weep, but the tears wouldn't come. What kind of son couldn't shed tears for his father? He could feel them, thick and hot in his throat, but they were stuck there. He hoped they didn't all come out in a humiliating rush at the funeral.

It had felt like the right thing to do, coming out to the lake. His father would be glad that Lance had worn the Italian suit, and the shoes that had cost more than a month's rent on his Houston apartment. Olan would be glad to see him here like this, straddling easily the two things the older man had valued most—money and nature.

It was an odd combination, but Lance's father loved having money. Lots of it. And he took pride in the fact that he'd earned every penny himself, doing a man's work, not some sissified thing like banking or playing the stock market. He hadn't been the best father or husband in the world, but on his own terms, in his own way, he'd done what he set out to do.

And Lance had loved him.

After a time, Lance knew he had to get back to his mother's house. There were a hundred things left to do, and she'd want it all to be just right.

He took his time walking back to his car, trying to breathe and feel okay, instead of the weird shakiness that seemed to have overtaken him. Maybe he was just hungry.

Driving back into town on the frontage road, he passed a stranded car, hood up. It was an old Buick, the paint faded to a dead-leaf color. Lance looked at the clock on his dashboard, and realized he was even later than he thought. His mother would have expected him almost an hour ago. He picked up the cellular phone to call the sheriff, and glanced in the rearview mirror.

It was Tamara Flynn, cursing a blue streak if her

body language was any indication. He put the phone down and pulled over, backing up to within a few feet of her.

She was so touchable, Lance thought, getting out of his car. Her thick dark hair lay on her shoulders, glossy and touchable in the early-morning sunlight. He let his gaze wander over her body, admiring the fit of jeans so old, he guessed she might have worn them in high school. It wasn't a fashionable sort of worn, but a patched and crossed-fingers type. And the effect of soft denim against her thighs and round, pretty bottom was unbelievably erotic.

Yesterday, he'd noticed her vivid green eyes and wariness, her work-worn hands. Today, he admired the neat, perfectly formed shape of her breasts, and her sleek waist and long legs, and he wanted to touch her. All over. Very slowly.

Judging by the look on her face as he approached, a little of the same thing was in her mind. Her gaze washed from his head to his toes, then back up again more slowly. The faintest hint of shock showed in her face.

She hid it fast enough. That pretty soft mouth went tight. "You again," she said with exasperation. "Are you following me around?"

Lance chuckled. "Not at all, sugar. Maybe I'm just your guardian angel."

"Some angel," she said with a frown. "I look like a tramp with this black eye."

A thread of regret wound through him. A purple-and-black-and-green bruise decorated her eye and the cheek below. He made a sympathetic face. "That's pretty nasty.'' Unable to resist, he added, ''You should have used that steak. It would have helped.''

''Right.'' She sighed in barely suppressed frustration. ''Is there any chance you can give me a lift to the community college?'' She looked at her watch. ''I have a test in exactly—'' she looked at her watch, a sensible thing on a thin black strap ''—twenty minutes. I don't have time to figure out what's wrong with this stupid car right now.''

''Careful,'' he said, bending toward the engine. ''You don't want her to hear you.''

''Trust me, that's mild in comparison to some of the things I've said.''

''Well, no wonder, then. She's probably trying to teach you a lesson.''

''She?''

''All engines are she,'' he said with a grin. ''Don't you know that?''

''Okay. She. And she heard me saying bad things about her, so she's misbehaving. You still didn't answer me. Can you give me a ride to school?''

''Hang on.'' He noticed with approval that there was no oil leaking anywhere inside the engine, and someone had taught her to keep things clean inside. Rare for a woman. ''What did she do?''

''There was a strange noise, like a big knock, and I lost all power.''

''Uh-oh.'' Lance hesitated for only a second before sticking his hand into the bowels of the car.

''Oh, don't mess up your suit!'' she protested.

Lance lifted his head and winked. ''Real men don't worry about suits, sugar.'' The truth was, he was pretty sure what the problem was, and the engine was so clean, it wasn't a problem. He wiggled the spark plug wires blindly, and found what he was looking for. One hung in empty space. "Okay. It's nothing serious. Just a thrown spark plug." He closed the hood. "Hop in my car, and I'll run you to school."

"Thank you." Picking a worn backpack up off the ground, she flung it over her shoulder, and headed up the road at a good pace. Her hair shifted smoothly, glimmering and shining.

He hurried to catch up. In the car, he said, "Reach in the glove box and get me that red rag, will you?"

She did, taking the greasy cloth out with two fingers. The smell of lemon-scented industrial cleaner filled the car.

He wiped his hands. "I'll send somebody out here to fix that for you. Let me have your keys."

"That isn't necessary." She folded her hands primly in her lap and looked straight ahead. "I'll manage."

"You're as prickly as a porcupine, you know? What made you so mean?"

That surprised her. Her head snapped around, and the green eyes flashed. "I'm not mean."

He grinned. "You are to me."

"It's not mean. I'm just not swooning in your presence, and I'm sure that's what you're used to."

"Is that right?" He rested one arm on the steering wheel. In profile, her nose was as straight as a blade of bluegrass, making her mouth below look all the more plush and inviting and soft. Her chin jutted ever so slightly upward as she steadfastly ignored him, and he let his gaze drop lower, to the smooth skin showing above her blouse, and the delicious roundness of breasts. Perfect breasts. Not too big, not too small. Very touchable.

"What *would* make you swoon, Tamara?" he asked in his best, most liquid voice.

It worked. At least a little. She crossed her arms as if in protection. "Getting to school on time would top my list at the moment."

"So if I get you there on time," he said, starting the engine, "you'll swoon?"

In exasperation, she sighed. "I'm really not the swooning sort of person."

He laughed, putting the car in gear. "Honey, all women can swoon." He pulled out and gave her a sideways glance, catching a reluctant tail of a smile on her mouth. "Trust me."

It was a test, Tamara told herself. A test to see if she really did have what it took to raise herself out of the pit she was in, and get on with some kind of real life. The universe was testing her mettle.

And what a test.

Yesterday, Lance had made her think of a steak, a homegrown, All-American beefsteak, thick and juicy. This morning he smelled of after-shave and soap. The hair at his collar was still damp from a shower, and his jaw showed a tiny nick from shaving. Tamara thought of Black Forest cake, sinfully delicious and far too rich for her tastes.

Food images. That wasn't terribly difficult to figure out. She was practically starving.

She took a long breath and let it go slowly. It didn't help much. From the corner of her eye, she saw his hand on the steering wheel, strong and square and dark. When he said, "swoon," it had been his hands she'd thought of, his hands gliding over her body with expertise and attention to detail.

The fresh-man smell filled her head. Impossible. This whole thing was impossible. It was hilarious that she'd even imagined she could even attempt to seduce such a man.

"What's your test in?" he asked.

Her heart nearly stopped dead. "Pardon?"

He looked at her, a secret dancing in those bright blue eyes. "Your test. What is your test this morning?"

"Oh." A tinge of heat moved on her jaw. "Accounting." She pointed at an intersection. "Turn left up there."

"I know where the college is, honey. I'm a native of this town, and it's not like anything is hidden." He changed lanes and took a swig of coffee from a thermal cup. "You like it?"

"Yes," she lied.

"You don't strike me as the accounting type."

"Oh." Maybe if she answered in monosyllables he'd stop talking in that warm, teasing voice and the little shivers on her arms would cease.

"No," he said, pulling into the parking lot at the school. "You seem like you'd be into all those poets, Byron and Whitfield—"

"Whitman."

"Right. And Shakespeare." He stopped the car in front of the front doors and gave her a wicked grin. "Maybe John Donne."

Tamara couldn't help herself. She stared at him. "You know Donne?"

Wickedness winked in his eyes. "'Love's mysteries in souls do grow, but yet the body is his book.'" He put an arm along the back of the seat and leaned toward her. "Does poetry make you swoon?"

It did. And he knew it. Tamara sat rooted to her seat, her ears awash with the sound of his voice shaping those elegant words. He edged forward and his eyes touched her mouth. His sun-burnished face filled her whole vision, with the sensual, mobile mouth at the center.

He was very close, and he smelled like heaven, and his mouth moved infinitely closer. She felt his breath whisper over her lower lip. Her heart pinched as if a huge heel were bearing down on it, and still she couldn't move.

And there, so close, millimeters from kissing her, he said, "You'd better get to class, honey, before you're late."

Tamara bolted, yanking open the door, half tumbling out, the little hairs on the back of her neck standing on end the way they did when she had to go up the basement steps in the dark, sure there were ghosts and demons and evil spirits on her heels. "Thank you," she said.

"Tamara."

She swallowed. "What?"

"Let me have your keys. It takes two dollars and three minutes to change a spark plug, and I'm guessing you have no idea how to do it." He pointed to a parking lot. "I'll leave it right over there, the keys in the glove box. You can pay me back next time I'm in the Wild Moose."

She couldn't bear one more second of looking at

him. Rather than argue, Tamara reached into her purse, dug out the keys and tossed them at him. "Thanks for the ride," she said, and bolted for class.

Chapter Four

She flunked her test. She got into class, flustered and rushed, only moments before the instructor passed out the forms. When she saw the sheet of questions, she realized she had studied the wrong chapter. Her heart sunk. She knew none of the answers on this test. Not even one, though she made educated guesses on a few.

And the day went downhill from there. In business administration, the teacher sprang news of an elaborate project that would be due in three weeks, an analysis of a corporation that would entail massive amounts of research. She grabbed a granola bar before statistics, which improved her mood marginally. The instructor handed her an envelope as she came in. Seeing the pink slip inside, she was afraid it was going to be a "see me after class" message, and couldn't think what she might have done wrong.

Instead, it was a scrawled note from Lance. He'd picked up her car, but it was more than a spark plug, and he'd taken the car to his mechanic. He'd left his own car for her use this afternoon. "Don't curse at her," he wrote, and signed his name.

She held the key in the palm of her hand as if it were a five-inch field spider. Drive his car? Sit in that fast, bad car and be seen in it? Not in this lifetime.

But in the end, she had no choice. It was her only day off this week, and she had to get her paycheck, then get some groceries in the house or they'd be eating peanut butter crackers for supper.

Safely in the car, away from the pressures of the day, Tamara bent her head and let herself cry. She felt frazzled and hassled and unable to cope. Her Buick, ugly and old as it was, was the only car she had, and if the repair bill was too steep, she wouldn't be able to do anything about it.

Which meant she'd probably have to drop out of school this semester.

She allowed herself five minutes to gnash her teeth and imagine the worst, then lifted her head and dried her tears with a tissue she found in the bottom of her purse. She checked for smeared mascara in the rearview mirror, and gave herself a stern glare. "Lighten up, Tamara Flynn." In her mother's Southern drawl, she said, "Where there's a will, there's a way."

It made her feel better. With new resolve, she turned the key in the ignition of the car and listened to it catch with a quiet roar. It handled like a dream, responding to her every little command like a dutiful soldier, carrying her down the highway with speed and smooth power. A cassette tape hung out of the stereo, and she impulsively pushed it in and turned it on. She expected George Thorogood or some other bad-boy of rock and roll, but it was Bonnie Raitt, singing "Louise."

The day was clear and cool, bright as only mountain autumns can be. Tamara rolled the window down and turned up the music, and let the wind blow her hair around as she sang along. The furry green of pines and blazing gold of aspens whizzed by. Sunlight poured from a sky as blue as turquoise.

What a car! she thought with amusement, pulling smoothly into the day care to pick up Cody. Wouldn't he get a kick out of it?

It was only as she got out and cheerfully slammed the door with a thunk that she noticed the long line of cars ribboning up the road toward Louise Forrest's house.

The funeral was today. That was why Lance had been dressed up this morning, and why he could let her use his car. With a thick sense of guilt, she followed the progress of the limo in front, wondering if Lance had loved his father. If he would miss him.

If he would love his son, the grandson of the man they buried today.

Louise served and chatted with the gathered well-wishers—nearly everyone in town. A headache pounded lightly at her temples, pervasive and not unexpected. The past few days had been a strain for all of them.

She eyed her sons carefully. Tyler sat in the rocker in the living room, reading a story to his son Curtis, who was sleepily sucking his thumb, his eyelids drooping as he valiantly fought to stay awake. Louise smiled. What a doll that child was!

Jake was making time with the barely dry-behind-the-ears daughter of a town councilman, a skinny blonde who'd been known to date mainly ski instructors the past few years. Judging by the gleam in her eyes, Jake was her next prey. Or she was his. Louise scowled. Today she didn't care. She was too tired.

She couldn't find Lance at first, but found him at last on the deck that jutted out over a hundred-foot drop into the valley. Wind from below blew his hair into disorder, tumbling it onto his collar in bright points. She closed the glass door behind her, and joined him at the rail.

"How are you, honey?" she asked, putting her hand on his broad back. The jacket of his expensive suit had been discarded, and she felt his extraordinary heat through the light cotton shirt. When he'd been a baby, she'd had to wait until his temperature was 102 before she called a doctor. His natural thermometer was just set high.

He roused himself, as if returning from a long way off. "I'm all right," he said, blinking. "You?"

"I'm tired," she admitted. "But we're almost through it all now."

Lance took her hand, clasping it between both of his. This was her sweet son—the little lover. As a child, he'd come downstairs in the morning and found her wherever she was, to give her a hug, first thing. Even as a teenager, he'd take her arm when they were out shopping, and put his arm around her when he introduced her to his friends. It was a rare thing in a man.

"I miss him already," he said now in a rough voice.

"I know you do." She brushed a lock of hair from his face. He'd been so stoic at the funeral, she worried about him. "You had a real special relationship with him. A man who is loved by his son can't have lived too bad a life."

Lance nodded, and she saw his eyes glimmer with unshed tears. He swallowed, lifting his head to the wide mountain sky, and she patted his hand.

"I'll leave you alone. No matter what your daddy said about boys and tears, I reckon even he would be honored right now."

She left him without looking back. It would be harder for Lance than for any of them. She had to be sure he had plenty of chances to grieve, get it out in the open where it wouldn't fester and poison him. She'd seen that festering happen with Tyler, and she wouldn't lose another son to it.

Tamara picked up her check and bought Cody his treat-night supper—a hamburger, shake and French fries from the local hamburger stand. Once he'd eaten, they stopped at the grocery store, where he picked out the words he'd learned to read. "Mommy, is that 'sale'?" "Mommy, is that 'fish'?" "Mommy, is that 'diet'?"

She nodded distractedly most of the time. Although he was only four, he'd been able to pick out most of the letters in the alphabet when he was two, and had been counting to a hundred for more than a year. It didn't surprise her anymore that he was teaching himself to read. Her mother had once told her that Valerie's father was the smartest man in Choctaw, Arkansas. Cody had evidently inherited his brains.

In the spice aisle, she bent over, looking for lemon pepper. Behind her, Cody chanted in his usual way, making comments on whatever he saw. And in her usual way, she said, "Mmm-hmm," every so often without really hearing.

But suddenly, his words penetrated, and she looked up, stunned. He was chanting the names of spices. "Nutmeg, nutmeg, nutmeg. Salt, salt, salt." He paused and frowned. "Carmamom." The sound pleased him. "Carma*mom*, carmamom, carma*mom*."

When he noticed Tamara looking at him, his impish little face wreathed itself in a smile. "Carma*mom!*"

"Cody," she said, standing, "are you reading the labels on the bottles?"

"Yep." He swung his feet and cocked his head. "Some are hard."

"Which one is hard?" She pulled the basket close to the shelves.

"That one." He pointed to a bottle of Italian seasoning.

Feeling a queer sense of excitement, Tamara forced herself to be calm as she pointed to another bottle. "How about this one?"

He leaned forward against the silver handle of the shopping basket and made little gestures with his mouth, murmuring under his breath. "Pop-py!" he cried. "Pop-py, pop-py, pop-py. Hey!" he cried. "That's almost pepper!" He pointed to the can nearby. "Black pepper." With a serious expression he added, "I already know the color words."

With a happy little giggle, Tamara took his face in

her palms and kissed his nose. "You are so smart,"
she said. "I didn't know you could read so well!"

He leaned on the bar. "I can't read books so good.
There's too many words."

"Oh, there are many books with only a few words
in them. I'll find you some, okay?"

"Okay." With a coy little expression, he said, "Can
we get some Power Rangers now?"

"Sorry, kid. Still can't afford one today. Maybe
next week. How about some cookies instead?"

He sighed. "Okay."

On the way home, she stopped at a discount store
and got several beginning readers for Cody. At the
checkout was a display of inexpensive classical CDs.
Impulsively she plucked out one of Vienna waltzes, as
a treat for herself. Maybe it hadn't been such a bad
day after all.

She had no real stereo system, but couldn't stand to
have no way to play music, and two years ago had
splurged on a boom box at an after-Christmas sale.
Happily, once they got home, she put the CD on and
started putting away her groceries.

"Turn it *up*, Mommy!" Cody cried, running into
the kitchen. "This is happy music!"

With a chuckle, she did just that. Cody spun and
whirled all over the living room, and she watched him
with a deep sense of satisfaction as she stowed the
perishables. Then, leaving the rest for later, she rushed
into the living room and scooped him up. "We can
dance together!"

She turned up the volume another notch, and spun
around with her son. The music, so rich and wild and
yes, happy, washed away the strain of her bad day.

Holding the precious, laughing body of her son in her arms, it all seemed worth it—losing college and Eric and having to be poor again when that was the one thing she'd vowed to avoid.

It was worth it. A thousand times over.

Lance could hear the music as soon as he turned off Tamara's car in her driveway. It was the "Blue Danube Waltz," floating out on waves of fairy-tale sound into the trees and the gathering dusk. In the living room she had turned a lamp on against the darkness, but had neglected to pull the curtains. He could see her plainly through the wide front window, dancing with her son. The little boy leaned back suddenly, letting his head fall, and Tamara spun him around. The boy's hair fluttered like the fringe on a yellow scarf.

Lance didn't move. He stood by the car, feeling somehow winded. It didn't occur to him to be ashamed of spying on them. He was simply entranced by the picture they made. As he watched, Tamara put her son on his feet, and led a march around the living room to the sound of the drums. Then the boy led. And when the swirling started again, they spun around side by side, arms out to the side. Lance found his attention snagged by the sight of her dark, sleek hair swinging in a bell around her shoulders.

Watching them, the sense of brittleness that had surrounded Lance all day ebbed, and he felt only very tired and empty. He might have stood there all evening, immobile, but a car came down the road, spitting gravel from the shoulder. Shaken from his trance, he went to the door and rang the bell.

Cody flung open the door. "Hey, the forest man!"

he said. The blond locks were tousled, and for a single moment, Lance was reminded of his brother Tyler. Ty's hair was lighter, but he'd been impish like this.

Hard to believe now. Lance doubted there was a more serious person on the planet.

"Hi there," Lance said. "Can I talk to your mom, please?"

He waited on the porch this time, unwilling to invade her private time with her child. Tamara came right to the door. Her cheeks were flushed a bright rosy color. "Oh, hi!" she said, pushing open the screen door. "Come in. Things are a mess, but... well, just come on."

As he stepped in, the next waltz came on, deafeningly loud. "Cody, turn that down for me, please." She looked at Lance. "Sorry. We got a little carried away."

He tried to find a smile, but it felt like only a shadow. "I saw you from outside. Looked like fun."

"Come in and sit down," she said. "Can I get you a cup of tea or something? I don't keep liquor or beer, but we have other things."

To his surprise, he settled on the couch. It was worn and comfortable, covered with a bright blanket. "I can't stay long. But maybe a cup of tea would be nice."

"Stay right there. I'll get it."

Cody had turned down the music, and now came over and sat down on the couch next to him. The boy pretended not to be interested. He sat close to the edge and swung his feet, his little hands in his lap, like a maiden aunt sitting with company.

Lance had practice making small talk with little ones. "You go to school yet?" he asked.

"No. Not real school. Only preschool." He brightened. "But I can read. Wanna see?"

"Sure." Lance chuckled.

Cody jumped down and scuttled over to the table. He brought back a stack of Dr. Seuss books. Lance guessed he'd been read to often, and had memorized the text of one or another of them. Cody held them out awkwardly, using his knee to keep from dropping the whole stack. "Which one do you want?"

"Let me help you, kiddo." Lance propped the books up on his palms. "You pick."

Cody looked at them carefully. "This one has mommy in it. I know that word pretty good."

Lance put the others on the table and let Cody crawl up next to him. The boy felt warm against him. The painful ache in his chest somehow eased with the contact, and he dropped his arm around the child. "Whenever you're ready."

"I hafta go slow, though," Cody said earnestly, his big blue eyes wide. "And you might have to help me with some words."

"I can do that."

Cody flipped open the book to a page in the middle and put his finger on the first word. "I don't know this one," he said.

"'Are,'" Lance said.

"Are you mmmm-mmm—eeee mommy?'" he said haltingly. "Oh! 'Are you *my* mommy?'"

"Good."

"That's not his mommy, I don't think," Cody said with a frown. "A bird needs a bird mommy."

Lance chuckled. "You're right."

Cody read the page, and by the way he stumbled and sounded out words according to the way they looked, Lance realized he wasn't reciting, but actually reading. At the end of the page, he said, "I'm very impressed, Cody. How old are you?"

"Four."

Tamara came back into the room, bearing a neat little wooden tray with a teapot in a cozy, a bowl of sugar and pitcher of milk, and two cups. "He's almost four and a half," she said.

"Mommy, I read this whole page!" he said.

"Very good, honey." She put the tray on the coffee table. "Why don't you go and play in your room now for a little while? I'll give you a bath later."

"Can I take my books?"

"Of course. They're yours."

Cody gathered the slippery books close to his chest. "Bye," he said.

"Bye. Thanks for reading to me."

Cody nodded and ran off to his room.

"Cute kid," Lance said. "Are you teaching him to read?"

Tamara straightened, looking after her son with a perplexed expression. "No. He has little magnetic letters on the fridge, and he watches 'Sesame Street' all the time, so he must have started putting them together in his head somehow." She shook her head, and gave him a smile that was very sweet. "I only realized this afternoon that he was really reading, not just picking out a word here and there."

Her whole attitude tonight was quite different from

what it had been the other times he'd seen her. She seemed kinder, warmer, not so bristly.

But maybe it was because he was putting out something different tonight. He had no energy left to flirt or tease or come on to her. When she handed him a cup of tea, he felt only grateful. "Thanks," he said.

"You're welcome." She poured herself a cup, and then looked at him earnestly. Gone were the harsh, tight lines around her mouth, the wariness in her eyes. "Lance, it was very kind of you to help me this morning."

"Glad to do it. No big deal."

"It was a big deal." She took a breath. "It was your father's funeral today, wasn't it?"

He looked down into his cup. The herb tea was a deep, rich red. "Yeah. It was."

"If I'd known, I would never have asked for a favor."

"You wouldn't have needed to take your test?"

"Of course I would have. But I just—I feel kind of bad. I'm sorry for your loss."

That thick, unbearable weight sunk against his chest again. "Thanks," he said, and heard how rough his voice sounded.

"I hope you don't mind me saying so, but you don't look very good tonight. Can I do something?"

If he hadn't been so damned worn-out, he would have summoned up something suggestive to counter that. Instead, to his horror, he felt the long-held tears in his throat suddenly rise. "No," he said abruptly. He put the tea aside and stood up, feeling a panicked need to get out of there before he completely humiliated himself. "No, I'm fine."

He rushed toward the door, blindly, without thought, certain of only one thing. Something about this warm house and the comfort of tea and a little boy's warmth against his side had destroyed his defenses, and he had to get out of there.

Now.

Chapter Five

Stunned, Tamara watched Lance jump up and bolt for the door. He was out on the porch before she managed to collect herself enough to go after him. "Lance!" she called, going through the door.

He stopped in the yard, his back to her. And for one tiny moment, Tamara couldn't help but admire the picture he made against the gilding of the last sunlight. His hair, those broad shoulders set in such stiff lines, the almost inhumanly perfect rear end.

Desire, pure and plain, filled her. She pushed it aside, aware that he needed something a lot more satisfying than a roll in the hay. Like maybe a friend. Or a shoulder to cry on.

She ran lightly down the steps and stopped next to him, instinctively reaching out to put her hand on his arm. He flinched. "I'm okay," he said gruffly.

"Well, if you say so," Tamara replied with a chuckle. "But if you were in my bar, I'd recommend a good shot of whiskey."

It worked. He gave her a quick, rueful glance. "I've been doing pretty good right up till this minute." With a rough swipe of his forearm, he rubbed his face. "I guess I'm just tired now. Oughta just get home before I make a total fool of myself."

His half smile was filled with heartbreaking bravado. For one evening, Tamara could ignore the past, and just live in the present. "I have a better idea," she said, firmly taking his arm. "I haven't had any supper, and I was going to make some French onion soup. It doesn't take long. Why don't you let me fix you some, too?"

He hesitated.

She tugged a little. "C'mon. Let me repay your kindness to me today."

He looked at her for a long, silent time, the dark blue eyes filled with hesitance and sorrow and exhaustion. The exhaustion won. "I think I'd like that."

True to her promise, the soup took only a half hour. Lance wandered into Cody's room while she cooked, and she heard them building something out of Lego blocks. Cody had collected the parts for a castle, and he loved to build the tower, with little Lego-men guards on top, but he needed an adult to help him. And much as she liked playing with him, Tamara did not often have time.

Listening to the soft conversation between the man and his son, Tamara wondered again if she were wrong to keep this knowledge from Lance. Whether he had intended to do it or not, he'd planted a child, and that child was bright and warm and wonderful. Especially in light of his very plain grief, perhaps the knowledge that he had a son might ease the sorrow.

Shredding cheese, she frowned. He probably did have a right to know. But if she told him, she'd have to deal with the very real and awkward issues of custody.

As the ramifications of that thought fully penetrated for the first time, the air left Tamara's lungs. What if Lance, in retribution or anger or even *love*, took Cody away from her?

She had officially adopted her nephew, but a blood father, especially one who had had no knowledge of the birth of his son, might have a higher claim. Especially a father with as much power as a Forrest commanded in this tightly knit mountain community.

Breathless, she sat down, the cheese grater still in her hands. Shreds of Parmesan drifted over the knees of her jeans and she brushed them off distractedly. How had she never considered this angle before? That Lance Forrest, if he knew, might take her son from her?

A rich, low man-laugh rolled out of the back bedroom, punctuated with the higher giggle of a boy. The sound seemed suddenly ominous to Tamara. To have worked so hard, and given up so much, only to lose him?

No.

To safeguard her interests, she had to talk to a lawyer. She had no idea how she would manage to pay for the services of one, but somehow, she had to find a way. She needed to be prepared, just in case....

In the bedroom, a tower of Lego blocks fell over with a crash, and Cody shrieked with glee. The sound broke into Tamara's frightened reverie. A smell of scorching onions penetrated and she jumped up to stir them.

Taking a deep breath, she calmed her racing thoughts. Lance Forrest was no more likely to steal Cody away than he was to marry a dowdy spinster. He was footloose and liked it that way. He wouldn't tie himself down to anything or anyone.

Or at least that's what she'd always believed. Tonight, looking so broken, she had cause to wonder. Maybe he wasn't quite the hellion she believed. Maybe his reputation was ill deserved.

Then she thought of Valerie. No, Lance had earned every word of his wild-man reputation.

So he likely wouldn't take Cody away from her, simply because it would mean tying himself down.

But sooner or later, Lance was bound to put two and two together and remember that Tamara was Valerie's cousin. He'd remember that wild Christmastime affair, and start to wonder. Or she would be in public somewhere, and run into Lance with his nephew Curtis, who was almost a twin of his cousin Cody. Tamara went to great pains to keep Cody out of Louise Forrest's sight. A grandmother would notice immediately the resemblance between the two boys.

So perhaps, just to be safe, Tamara needed to be clear on her legal rights before she told Lance about his son. Sooner or later, he was going to find out the truth, and it might be best for everyone if he heard the news from her own lips.

* * *

After scaring herself silly with thoughts of Lance taking Cody away from her, Tamara regretted her decision to invite him to stay. And yet, he showed no signs of hurrying off. He ate the soup with genuine hunger. When Tamara said she needed to give Cody his bath and get him to bed, hoping Lance would take the hint and leave, he only stood up and started collecting the dishes. "How about if I wash these up for you, then?"

"Oh, that's not necessary," she protested. "I know how tired you must be."

"No trouble," he said, and walked toward the kitchen.

Tamara gave up. She hurried Cody through his bath, and read him one story, then tucked him in, and rushed back into the kitchen. She would tell him she had to study. That she had—

But he wasn't in the kitchen, although all the dishes were neatly stacked on the drainboard. He'd even wiped the counters and stove, something Eric had always missed. "Lance?" she called.

No answer. She wandered out through the dining room of the small bungalow and into the living room. And there he was, sprawled in her comfortable, overstuffed recliner, sound asleep. Tamara stopped, putting a hand to her stomach, pierced by his rough, vulnerable beauty.

Yellow light spilled over him from the floor lamp, illuminating the bright streaks in his uncut hair, and catching the faint bristles of beard beginning to show on his jaw after the long day. She followed a finger of light from his high brow, down his straight nose, to the edge of his lower lip. His head was cast sideways, showing the line of his strong brown throat, and the triangle of chest above his shirt. Lamplight plucked a faint scattering of gilded hair on his chest.

He breathed deeply, slowly, one hand on his chest, his long, jean-clad legs flung out over the footrest.

Tamara filled her eyes, letting wonder creep over her. He was the kind of man a woman would make up, the kind of man a woman would fashion for her own pleasure. Thick hair to run her fingers through, a mobile mouth made for half-cocked grins, the lips shaped for kissing a woman for a long, long time, the strong, hard body made for touching and embracing and making long, lazy love.

Standing in the doorway, Tamara found it far too easy to imagine herself stretched out over that long, lean length, her body pressed into his—

Oh, Valerie! she thought. *No wonder you fell so hard!*

With a rueful smile, she shook her head at herself. It had been too long since she'd had a lover. Way too long. That was the trouble with sex—you could do without forever as long as you never tasted the fruit. Once tasted, it was always missed.

It was something she'd learned by watching Valerie, actually. And she'd been careful to preserve her innocence until college. Until she met Eric, who had seemed to share her goals and dreams. She'd never regretted either waiting or deciding to at last sample the fruits of the flesh.

Until now. Now it seemed impossible she'd gone four years without making love. Without letting herself even dream of it.

From the couch, she took the blanket, and covered Lance with it. He barely moved. Up close, she could see the etching of weariness around his mouth, the deepening of strain around his eyes. Tamara remembered the strain of her mother's funeral, and how completely drained she'd felt that night. It would hurt nothing to let him sleep here for an hour or two. She had to study anyway. When she was finished, she would awaken him and send him on his way.

But as she settled at the table, she noticed she sat facing him, so she could watch him. It was bound to make studying statistics a little bit more pleasant, much like playing sonatas to ease the pain of accounting or reading business administration at the park so the sunshine took away the boredom.

A wry grin twisted her mouth as she flipped open the textbook. "You're a hussy at heart, Flynn," she said under her breath, and lifted her eyes to the gilded picture of Lance Forrest lying asleep in her chair.

There were worse things, she thought, and applied herself to her studies.

A faint, faraway ringing yanked Lance from his fathomless, dreamless sleep, and he sat up abruptly, the recliner slamming closed. His arm tangled in a blanket, and his foot was asleep, and—where the hell was he?

He blinked hard, trying to erase the fuzziness on him, and spied a toy car on the floor. Oh, yeah. Tamara's house. He must have fallen asleep.

He didn't see her, but the evidence of her was scattered all over the table—notebooks and papers and pencils and textbooks. From the kitchen, he heard her voice, soft and pleasant, like wind in the trees on a summer morning.

With effort, he untangled himself from the blanket and leaned back once again in the chair. The woman was going to think he was a basket case—he'd nearly wept right out there in the yard, and then he'd fallen asleep in her chair.

Not exactly his usual modus operandi.

Somehow, he couldn't find it in him to care. His limbs felt heavy and thick, and he couldn't summon the energy to move just yet. It was so comfortable here. Not just in the chair, but in the house.

It was obvious she had little money—the couch had worn places that the blanket had covered, and nothing matched. But there were framed prints on the walls— maybe cut from a calendar of Impressionist art, judging by the matched size and spirit of them. He liked the way she had hung them, not all in a line, but scattered high and low over the whole wall. In one corner was a basket of dried mountain plants, attractively arranged with a branch of aspen coins providing the centerpiece. There were small lamps here and there, creating inviting islands of light. The house even smelled good, like spice and cooking and bubble bath.

It was comfortable. Almost protective.

He'd forgotten how warm a woman could be. He'd forgotten that countrywomen naturally saw to the feeding and care of any weary town person in her path, as Tamara had tended him tonight. He was almost absurdly grateful.

She came back in the room, not noticing he was awake. She glanced at her watch and sighed. So pretty, he thought blurrily. So feminine and strong all at once. "Hey," he said. "How did that test go this morning?"

"You're awake!" She brushed a lock of hair from

her face, tugged down her simple T-shirt, crossed her arms. He doubted that she realized how nicely the pose displayed her round, high breasts. Until she noticed him noticing. She dropped her arms, put her hands on her hips, didn't like that, either, and shifted from foot to foot.

Still sprawled backward in the chair, Lance grinned very slowly. She was flustered. That must mean she liked him a little bit. Women didn't bother to get flustered around men they didn't like.

"Must not have done too well, if you won't even tell me what you got," he said.

"I flunked." The words were without rancor, and she inclined her head. "To tell you the truth, I was going to blame you, Mr. Forrest, but I didn't study the right chapter."

She looked good. Like a Sunday afternoon in a meadow. Like a good bottle of wine. Like everything calm and soothing in the world.

Like good sex.

Sleepily he blinked. Yeah, that, too. That sweet mouth, her pretty breasts, that hint of fury and passion in her green eyes. Unless he missed his guess—and if he knew anything, it was women—she hid a very passionate nature behind all that no-nonsense busyness.

"Blame me?" he echoed with a smile. "What did I do?"

She looked away, tracing the edge of her book with a fingernail. The thick hair fell over her face, hiding it, but he saw the blush pinken the skin of her chest. Ah-ha.

"Nothing. I just wanted to blame someone." She

tossed her hair from her face. The pointed chin jutted upward. "But I was just dumb."

"Nah," he said, standing up. "Never that." In a couple of long strides, he closed the distance between them. He stopped in front of her, acting purely on instinct. Lifting one hand, he brushed his fingers over the greenish bruise that marked her face. "Maybe you were just distracted."

It was the second time he'd touched her. And for the second time, he noticed her skin was almost astonishingly soft and silky. Caught by the texture, he ran his fingers over her cheek. She didn't move away, but she lowered her gaze. He touched her thin eyelids, traced her eyebrows, which were as dark as her hair, and shaped like bird wings. "You must be part Indian, to have such dark hair."

"My father was half Choctaw." The response was automatic enough he knew she said it a lot.

A dizziness—maybe exhaustion or loss or simple appreciation—moved through him. She was as easy to enjoy as a dandelion growing in a forgotten lot. And like a dandelion, he suspected she had long and sturdy roots, a stubborn will to survive that would not be easily killed.

He lifted his other hand to her face and cupped the piquant shape between his palms, spreading his finger open so he could touch as much of that tender skin as possible. "Wow," he said, and couldn't think of anything else to add.

"What are you doing?" she whispered.

"I don't know," he admitted. "Your skin is so soft I just want to feel it. Do you mind?"

"Yes," she whispered. She raised her lids, revealing the dusky heat in her eyes. He doubted she knew that it showed so plainly, so alluringly. "Please don't," she said.

But her body betrayed her. She shivered a little and her lips looked suddenly moist and ready.

Lance kissed her. It was done with no thought, no planning. He just bent his head and tasted her lips. It seemed like such a simple thing, the obvious thing to do—bend his head and taste the roses of her lips.

But it wasn't simple. A bolt of something pure and clean and hot moved through him as their lips touched, a physical jolt as powerful as a plunge into the ocean. Her lips tasted faintly of lemon tea and salt, and they fit his with an extraordinary perfection, as if their mouths had been carved together, long ago in another world, and only now fit together again.

It was so unexpectedly satisfying that Lance didn't even feel any need to go within. There was enough just right there, in the sweetness of lips too long untouched—and hungry, by the way she returned the kiss—and the discovery of a mouth so flawlessly molded to his own. When he inclined his head, she moved the other way; when he moved, she moved.

Her hands came up to catch his wrists, as if to pull his hands away. But she didn't. She only curled those small cold fingers around his arms and held on. And he kissed her, and she kissed him back—small, delicate, nibbling kisses that explored this place and then another, kisses that grew longer and warmer and moister.

Before it could be too much, or he pushed farther than he wanted or she needed, Lance lifted his head. Still holding her face, he tasted his mouth with his tongue. "Mmm," he said, and was surprised at the husky sound of it.

She pulled free, her color high. "I think it's time for you to go."

"Yeah," he said. "So do I." He ran a hand through his hair, feeling how uncombed it was. Weariness made him unstable on his feet. God, he'd never been so tired! "Your car is fine now. You shouldn't have any problems."

Tamara dug in a backpack and came up with his keys. She put them in his hand. "What was wrong with it?"

There had actually been quite a lot wrong. The radiator had a crack and he'd had it replaced, but he knew she didn't have any money. He'd seen her panic this morning. One thing having money let him do was little things like this, without anybody ever having to know. It somehow made it better to have it in the first place, when so many people did not. "It wasn't much. The spark plug and some crossed wires. Joe got it fixed."

"Joe Moran?"

"Right. I paid him, so you can just pay me when you can. It was twenty-three dollars." He grinned. "Well, actually $23.09, if you want to be exact."

Visible relief broke on her face. "Good. I have it right here." She counted the bills from her wallet, and with a grin, plucked a dime to put on top. "So we're square."

He chuckled and pocketed the money. From the back of a chair, he took his jean jacket. "Don't forget, now. Cars don't like to be sworn at. You didn't swear at my darlin', now did you?"

"How could anyone swear at that car? It runs like an animal or something." She gave him a sheepish smile.

"Amazing, isn't she?" He put his jacket on. "I used to have one in high school, but a crazy woman trashed it when she got mad at me."

"Trashed it? How?"

"She took a hammer to the windows and the lights, and slit the tires." He frowned, remembering how wounded and furious he'd been, coming out of the school to find the car destroyed. "And as if that wasn't enough, she put holes all over the body with a screwdriver."

"Good grief! What was she so mad about?" Tamara was surprised. Valerie's version of their ill-fated romance had not included these things.

"I broke up with her." He shrugged. "That was about the fifth or sixth time I tried. She was crazy, that girl." He shook his head, remembering. "Crazy Valerie. I wonder what happened to her."

A sudden cold infused the room. "She died," Tamara said abruptly.

"What?"

Tamara's eyes glittered with a cold light, and her posture was definitely not friendly now. "Valerie Jensen, right? She drove herself off a cliff."

A pang touched him. "Poor kid. When did it happen?"

"A little over four years ago."

"That's really sad." Sobered, he remembered seeing her one Christmas. She'd seemed better then. Better enough that she drove him crazy in spite of himself. She'd always been a hot one.

Tamara's chilly silence finally penetrated. He glance over at her, and was surprised to see pure hatred on her face. "Hey, I didn't do it," he said, lightly. "I swear."

"Nobody said you did." Her words were dry and weary. "She was my cousin, Lance. I loved her."

He closed his eyes. "I'm sorry." He'd been planning to exit with an invitation to dinner, but maybe this wasn't exactly the best timing. "I guess I'll see you around," he said.

"Good night."

At the door, he hesitated, and looked back at her. Rigidly, she stood by the table, but her eyes were not quite so cold. "Thanks for supper," he said, and left, closing the door behind him.

Tamara sank wearily into the chair, her limbs trembling with the roller coaster of emotions she'd ridden tonight. Compassion, fear, desire, fondness and pure furious lust when he'd kissed her. Now a wild sense of betrayal and sorrow mixed with guilt.

Crazy Valerie.

What was she doing? From the moment he'd arrived in town, Tamara had been promising herself she'd find revenge. And what had she done instead? Laughed with him. Admired him. Wanted him.

She buried her face in her arms. Oh, yes, she wanted him. The kiss lingered like poison on her lips. His hands, so big and callused and gentle, clung in ghostly imprints to her cheeks. He was excruciatingly tender, and yet the promise of wild, pure pleasure was there in every tiny brush of his lips, his hands, his exploring, curious fingers.

Crazy Valerie.

No wonder Valerie had been so smitten. Tamara had been in his presence four times, and her head was already crammed full of erotic imaginings. He gave the impression of sinfulness, combined with a surprising sweetness, and a promise of long, playful, hedonistic sex.

What woman, with even one hormone left in her body, could resist that heady combination?

Crazy Valerie.

Tamara had no right to be thinking of him in this way. No right to betray her cousin's memory because she was lonely and Lance offered a respite from the daily grind.

She lifted her head, narrowing her eyes. He was charming and sexy and plainly liked women of all kinds, and had decided Tamara might be a nice diversion.

Valerie had likely thought he was a nice guy, too. Until she had got to know him. Until he broke her heart. Until he used her and left her—pregnant—sending Valerie over the edge.

Firmly, Tamara slammed her books closed. She'd do well to remember what had happened to Valerie. Maybe revenge was out of the question, since Tamara couldn't trust herself in his presence. But she wouldn't fall prey to his charm, either.

She'd just stay away from him.

Chapter Six

Friday night, Lance walked into the Wild Moose Inn. It was just past nine, and the evening was in full swing. A Bob Seger tune blasted from the jukebox, and there were couples moving on the small dance floor by the rest room.

He'd arranged to meet his brothers here for a drink, coaxing even reclusive Tyler into an evening on the town. Lance paused just inside the door, looking for them. The place was packed full of men in their best Friday-night jeans, and women in glitzy blouses made to show off their attributes to best advantage.

A fist of depression struck him, forcing the air from his lungs. Too much noise. Too many people. He hesitated, wondering if he ought to just turn around and go home. The apartment he'd taken was small and cheerless, without any personal touches thus far, but at least he wouldn't have to face anyone there.

Then he caught sight of Tamara behind the bar. A nearly audible sense of relief moved through his limbs in a whoosh, and caught; Lance let himself feast on the sight of her.

Somehow she managed to look both friendly and frazzled. Her dark hair was swept up into a loose knot that let wisps fall down her slim white neck. She moved efficiently, retrieving beers, taking money, laughing on time at a joke someone at the bar made.

She saw him. He lifted his chin in greeting, a smile ready on his lips. If Tamara were here, maybe the night wouldn't be such a trial. But in response to him, her face hardened, grew cold and distant. She returned his greeting with a faint, tight smile and turned her attention back to the man at the counter.

Lance frowned. In the two weeks since he'd last seen her, he'd thought of her often. More often, really, than was comfortable. Women didn't usually get under his skin, but Tamara seemed to have done just that. He couldn't stop remembering how comfortable she made him feel. How much at ease.

The kiss had ruined it. He'd known even when he'd done it that it was wrong. Wrong for her, anyway. The memory of that long, chaste press of lips lingered in his memory like golden honey.

Rubbing absently at the ache in his midsection, he spied his brothers way back in a dark corner. Lance joined them. "Are we in hiding back here?"

"Ty got here first," Jake said with a wry grin, shaking the tumbler of Scotch in his hands.

Ty had braided his pale, long hair, and had even shaved the wheat-colored grizzling of beard from his jaw. "We can move if you want." He shrugged. "It makes no difference to me. I just didn't want to have to make conversation with anybody.''

Lance grinned. "You're a hermit, man.''

"I'm here.'' Ty lifted a bottle of Guinness stout and scanned the room as if it were filled with dragons. "Don't know why you guys couldn't come up to my place.''

"Tyler, let me tell you something.'' Jake slid close and put his arm around Ty. He gestured with one long-fingered hand. "You see that table over there? We call those women. They're nice and soft, and good for what ails you.''

"Not interested.'' Tyler said. His mouth tilted in a faint, derisive smile. "But I'm guessing the blonde wants you bad, Jakey. Such a surprise.''

Lance glanced over his shoulder to see who they were talking about. Not far away was a table of five or six women, not a one past twenty-five. A couple of them were very pretty, a couple more not bad. One was quite heavy, and looked hopeful. The blonde Tyler mentioned was about twenty-two, dressed in a city style with a sleek haircut that marked her as one of the rich kids that vacationed up here. She cocked a smile toward them.

"Yeah, Jake, you got her.''

Jake lifted his glass in a toast, and the young woman returned the gesture. Jake said, "Excuse me, boys,'' and slid out of the booth.

Lance watched him. Jake's dark hair hadn't been cut in a long time, and his jaw was shadowed with a three-day beard. He wore a pair of jeans and boots, like a rancher, and a simple chambray shirt. The girls at the table visibly straightened at his approach. When he bent over to whisper in the blonde's ear, she blushed and went to dance with him.

"Damn," Tyler said. "He's a dog these days. I bet he's dated twenty-five different women since he hit town a month ago." Tyler lifted an eyebrow. "Thought that was your job."

"I'm too damned tired. Dad left a mess at the company."

"I'm not surprised. He was feeling pretty bad for about six months before he died. But you know Dad—doctors were for sissies."

The waitress stopped by and Lance ordered a beer. He looked at Jake, dancing and flirtatiously moving closer to the woman in his arms. In the uneven light from overhead, the gaunt hollows under his eyes and cheekbones were highlighted. "I'm worried about Jake," Lance said. "I wonder if he ever sleeps."

"Sure doesn't look like it." Tyler shook his head. "I used to hate all that military neatness, but it's too weird to see him like this."

"Wonder what happened?"

"Whatever it is, he's not talking." He fixed his pale gaze on Jake. "Must have been something big. You know he left the army with only four years to full retirement?"

Lance nodded. "What about you? How are you doing?"

Tyler shrugged. "Same old, same old. I just do what I do."

"Still not dating at all?" Ty's wife had died three years before, and he had rarely come down out of the mountains since.

"It's not that I made a vow or anything," Ty said,

his eyes clouding. "It's just that I haven't met a woman I wanted to date."

Lance knew better than to push. "I guess it just takes time. I bet you'll find somebody sooner or later." He grinned. "Of course, you have to actually talk to another woman every once in a while."

"I don't really want another woman." Tyler shrugged. "I'm just not interested."

The waitress brought the beer and Lance paid her. He glanced at the bar. Tamara worked steadfastly. Her blouse was a pretty green thing with a scoop neck, and he liked the way it made her look like a wistful romantic heroine. "You know the bartender?"

"Tamara. She used to work at the bank when she was in high school." Ty narrowed his eyes. "That's not the woman you're set on, is it?"

"What makes you think I'm set on anybody? I told you I've been too damned busy to do any kind of dating."

"You never drink here. I figured there had to be a woman involved when you suggested we come here."

Lance chuckled. "Well, maybe I did notice her a little bit."

"Not a good choice, man. For one thing, she's Valerie's cousin."

"I heard." He frowned. "How come nobody told me Valerie died, anyway?"

Tyler rubbed his face. "Must have just been overlooked. That was when Kara was pregnant, and we were all worried about Jake cleaning up after Desert Storm, and Dad started living with his mistress. Pretty rough year all the way around."

"I guess it was." He pursed his lips, watching Tamara turn out five margaritas, bam bam bam. Salt, ice, a whir in the blender, pour and garnish. Quick, clean, economy of motion. "She's not Valerie, though."

"No, she's not," Ty agreed. "That's the whole point. She doesn't need some fast-talking rebel to sweep her off her feet and leave her in the dust. She needs somebody stable and steady who is going to be a husband for her and a father to that boy of hers."

"Where is Cody's father, anyway?"

Ty shrugged. "No idea. I don't think anyone knows." He gave Lance a level, cold look. "I mean it, Lance. She's not the kind of fast woman you like."

Irritated, Lance stripped the beer bottle of its label. "Not everybody wants marriage every minute. Sometimes it's nice just to take a break and have a good time. It isn't like I go around pretending I'm something I'm not."

"Maybe not. Just don't lead her on."

Lance gave him a half grin. "Or what? You'll beat me up?"

Tyler grinned back. "I'll take a hammer to your windshield."

"Low blow." Lance shook his head and sighed. "I feel bad for Valerie, but that was one crazy woman."

"She was just crazy in love with you," Tyler said, tongue in cheek. The ordinarily sober eyes glinted with humor. "I remember when she wrote 'Valerie Loves Lance' with lipstick on the school windows." He laughed. "Remember?"

Lance winced. "Yep."

"And when she came to the house in the middle of the night and sang outside your window."

"Mmm-hmm."

Jake sat down. "Who, Valerie?"

Lance drank, wishing like hell this topic had never been started.

"We were reminiscing," Ty said. "Remembering Valerie fondly."

Jake laughed. "I remember the time she called the house every ten minutes, around the clock, for three days. And the time she showed up at that Halloween party?"

Lance ignored them, feeling a flush move over his cheeks. For two years, he'd gone with Valerie. They'd broken up at least forty times, only to get back together a day or a week or a month later. To say it had been tempestuous was like saying an earthquake broke a few glasses.

"C'mon," he finally protested. "I was sixteen and one raging hormone, and so was she."

Ty snorted. "I remember when I caught you guys in the barn."

"And there was the time in the locker room at school," Jake said, practically chortling.

"Excuse me, gentlemen," Lance said, standing. He made his way to the jukebox, hoping his brothers would have finished their parade of humiliating moments by the time he got back. Punching in numbers blindly, he remembered the craziness with a sense of bewilderment. It seemed like another life.

It was another life. He had, at times, honestly thought he was in love with Valerie. She was unbelievably beautiful, a cross between Vivien Leigh and Elizabeth Taylor, with a body like Marilyn Monroe.

But mainly, it had been sex. Wild sex, crazy sex,

the kind of drunken, rushing, dizzying sex only two hormonally crazed sixteen-year-olds could indulge.

When he'd come home at Christmas a few years ago, he'd been lonely and out of sorts, and had run into Valerie in a bar. The same thing had happened all over again—three weeks of pure, mindless, practically nonstop sex.

Hard to resist, but when her old tricks started, in little ways—her talk of marriage and children and settling down—Lance didn't wait for her to trash his car. He left town and didn't look back.

Lance pocketed the rest of his change and looked at Tamara. He guessed she might have reason to hold a grudge against him. He'd used Valerie. Maybe Tamara didn't understand that Valerie had used him right back. It had always been a two-way street.

A man came into the bar and sat down on a barstool. Tamara gave him a sincere smile, laughing at some joke he made, and served up a Tecate with lime.

Lance walked over to the man and clapped him on the back. "Hey, Alonzo! Let me buy you that drink." He shoved a five-dollar bill over the counter at Tamara.

Alonzo Chacon looked up with a grin. "Hey, boss."

Alonzo was a Mexican national who'd immigrated to Colorado two years before. Lance had just hired him to lead and teach a crew to make adobe bricks. Alonzo made them the old way, by hand and individually. With adobe in such high demand for the homes going up in the area, Lance knew he had a gold mine.

Alonzo's dark eyes crinkled in the wreath of lines wrought by fifty-plus years in the sun, and his thick black mustache shone in the low light. *"Gracias."*

Tamara took the money and made change without saying a word. Lance found himself watching her hungrily, the long long legs, the smooth sway of her hips and the faint, alluring movement of her breasts below the loose blouse. The green fabric made her eyes look like jade—deep and rich and mysterious.

"Hi, Tamara," he said. "How's your car?"

"Fine, thanks," she answered shortly, and turned away to wait on someone else.

He grinned ruefully at Alonzo, whose dark eyes glittered in amusement. "She not so nice to you," he said with a wink. "But I see her watching you a minute ago. D'you make her mad?"

"Afraid so," he admitted. "Trouble is, I can't quite figure out what I did." He gestured. "Come and join my brothers and I."

Agreeable, Alonzo picked up his beer. "Lead the way."

Lance peeled another five and left it on the bar as a tip, lifting one wicked brow at Alonzo, who nodded sagely.

Friday nights were always a zoo in the bar, which was why Tamara had to work them. No one had Friday nights off. Tonight, the restaurant next door was full of diners, and a flurry of waitresses moved in and out of the bar, calling out orders for margaritas and "Red Bulls," the house drink, made of vodka, cranberry juice, lemonade, and sweet and sour.

The bar, too, was packed, and a steady stream of music poured from the jukebox, a mix of old rock and roll and country that so marked the mountain towns. Tamara liked most of it—the Eagles and Allman

Brothers and old Jackson Browne tossed in the same set with Willie Nelson and a few, slow, dancing tunes.

Tonight, Tamara was thankful for the crowd. It kept her busy enough that she didn't eye Lance Forrest more than once every five minutes or so, and she got busy enough that for a good twenty minutes she almost forgot he was there.

He danced. A lot, and she thought it was telling he didn't seem to have to leave his table to do it. Women went to him, and he never turned any of them down.

Women approached Lance's brothers, too, but Lance was usually their first choice. Jake scared women a little—he was almost too good-looking, with those Mel Gibson blue eyes and the obvious scent of money that clung to the cut of his shirt and the watch on his wrist and the Scotch he drank.

And although Ty had a very sexy mountain man look, he didn't get up once, just sat in the darkest corner and nursed a Guinness for two hours. He got up and left after that, and Tamara felt a little sorry for him. Everyone knew he'd taken his wife's death very hard.

Not long after Ty cleared out, Jake left with the out-of-town blonde. Lance and Alonzo chatted awhile longer, obviously about something work related, because Alonzo came up and asked for paper and a pencil, which he took back to the table and used to sketch.

Then Alonzo, too, was on his way. Tamara's stomach gave a little jump when Lance stood up. Maybe he'd go, too, and she could stop feeling so tense.

But he didn't. He tossed his jean jacket over his shoulder and picked up his beer. Ambling with that set-the-streets-afire loose-limbed grace, he crossed the room. To the bar, where he settled with a faint smile on his lips. "Evening, sugar. Get me another beer, please?"

Without speaking, Tamara turned and fished one out of the cooler. Her hand trembled ever so slightly as she opened it and set it down beside him. She hoped he didn't notice.

It would all be a hell of a lot easier if he weren't so wretchedly, exquisitely perfect. The glimmer in his eye, that lean and sexy body, the cut of his face. It wasn't fair.

And it wasn't as if she were the only woman in the room to notice, either. A gaggle of woman in a corner booth eyed him, some covertly, one boldly. Tamara lifted her chin toward them. "I think you might be able to wrangle a dance out of one of those young ladies."

Lance grinned and lifted his beer lazily, taking a long pull before he put it down. "I never had to 'wrangle' a dance in my life." His eyes tilted mischievously. "I just go on out and claim one."

"I'm so impressed," she returned, her voice clearly claiming the opposite.

"I knew you would be." He glanced over his shoulder at the table of women. "I have a feeling they'd be a lot more so."

He left his beer on the bar and strolled over to the table. Tamara crossed her arms against the slightly sick feeling in her stomach, trying to guess which one he'd ask. There were two possibilities. A brunette in a turquoise blouse, with earrings beaded to match the beads on her shirt; and a slim, tiny blonde in a bare nothing of a dress. They both eyed him with avarice, shifting in their seats to display their attributes to best advantage.

Tamara was suddenly transported to a shopping mall in Denver, ten years before. She had been sitting with Valerie in a café open to the view of passerbys, and Valerie had preened just like this the entire time they sat there—pouting and leaning and tossing her dark, glossy hair to send it rippling over her snowy white and perfect shoulders.

Tamara had felt then what she felt now. As plain as rice. Even worse, tonight she felt the stickiness of sweet and sour mix on her skin, and the faint sheen of sweat on her brow, and the limpness of hair pinned up. She wished she owned a single item of alluring clothing. Just one blouse that might make her look like something other than a hardworking mother with no ready cash.

She didn't wait to see which of the two pretty women Lance picked, but grabbed a bar towel and vigorously began to wipe down surfaces. It was hours before they closed, but the more work she did now, the less she'd have to do later.

Turning her back to the room, she started wiping down liquor bottles, turning their labels to face front. In the mirror behind the bottles, she had a good view of Lance's broad back, covered in red plaid flannel. She tried not to look, but traitorously watched as the woman stood up. The brunette. No, must be the blonde. No, it was another girl entirely, the only one at the table she would not have imagined Lance to pick.

Her name was Marissa. Tamara knew her from school. She was pretty enough with thick, perfectly cut dark hair and big blue eyes. In coloring, at least, she was like Valerie.

But Marissa was quite, quite heavy. Not merely plump. Not Rubenesque. She wore flowing, pretty fabrics, and carried herself lightly, but there was no denying the fact that she was at least seventy-five pounds overweight. Maybe even a hundred.

Tamara dropped the pretense of watching in the mirror, and turned around. Marissa's face was wreathed in an attractive flush and as she followed Lance to the dance floor. He took her hand and gave her a dazzling version of his killer smile.

They danced. And danced and danced and danced. And against her will, Tamara was touched. It was a kindness to dance with the round girl, who'd been tapping her foot hopefully all evening. And they were well matched on the dance floor—moving wildly and cheerfully and exuberantly. Everyone watching had to smile.

When, winded and flushed and perspiring, they finally quit, Lance grabbed her arm as she started to return to her booth, and pointed to the bar. The girl laughed and nodded.

Tamara met them, a tight knot of something in her chest. "What would you like?" she asked, putting a napkin down.

"Hi!" Marissa said. "Weren't you in my accounting class last semester?"

"Yes. You were the one with the 4.0 average." Tamara smiled ruefully. "I was the one who flunked the final and had to repeat the class."

"Oh, no!" Marissa reached over the bar and put

her hand on Tamara's. "You should call me. I'm really good at it. I can help you if you want."

She really was astonishingly pretty. Skin like porcelain. Tamara wondered how she kept it so flawless. "Thanks."

Lance winked. "I've been telling Tamara she doesn't strike me as a math person. What do you think?"

"Oh, really?" Marissa smiled. "That's not something you can tell by looking at a person. Do you like numbers?"

Tamara allowed a reluctant smile. "No. But a person cannot support herself with an English degree."

"That's true."

"You can do anything you want to do," Lance said, shaking his head. "You just have to believe you can."

"Right. It's easy to say that when you're born with a silver spoon in your mouth," Tamara said. "Money makes everything easy."

To her surprise, Lance lowered his head, almost wincing. Oddly, Tamara felt a little ashamed of herself.

Marissa looked at Lance, then back to Tamara, a more sober look in her eye. "Anyone who has money will tell you that it doesn't do anything except make you feel guilty for not being happy or thin or perfect." She chuckled. "My father has more money than Trump, and what am I doing? Studying accounting at a community college in the wilds of Colorado!"

"I bet it drives him crazy," Lance said.

Marissa nodded cheerfully. "Bingo." Turning back to Tamara, she said, "I think I'd like a margarita. Lots of salt."

"Coming right up." Tamara moved away, feeling claustrophobic and left out and dismissed. A servant.

As she prepared the margarita, she mentally shook herself. What was wrong with her lately? All she ever did was feel sorry for herself. Poor pitiful Tamara, who had to make her own way in the world.

It got old after a while. She was beginning to sound like Valerie and her mother, who had taken the attitude that they'd been dealt a bad hand and the world had to make it up to them. That, as well as an incident with Valerie and a couple of boys behind the barn, had been the reason Tamara had been forbidden to associate with her cousin and aunt.

Her mother would be so ashamed of her tonight!

With special care, Tamara made the margarita, and grabbed a bottle of expensive beer Lance sometimes drank. She served them with a flourish. "These are on the house." She wiped her hands on a bar towel self-consciously. "My apologies."

Lance looked up, his dark blue eyes sober for once, searching. "You don't have to do that, Tamara."

"I want to. Enjoy."

She moved away to take the order of a waitress, leaving them some privacy. Wryly she imagined them discussing the trials of having to go to prep school and the strain of international travel.

For her part, she'd gladly trade places.

Or would she? Would she really have traded her own mother for Olan Forrest? Tamara's mother, who had passed away five years ago from cancer, had been a loving, cheerful woman whose only mistake had been an unexpected and devastating unwed pregnancy. She had made Tamara's life very rich with her songs and cooking and loving hands. She had always had time for Tamara, time to help with schoolwork or cooking lessons or a stroll in the park. When other girls complained that their mothers simply didn't understand them, Tamara had hugged the secret wonder of her mother to her closely.

In contrast, Olan Forrest, rich as he was, had been mean-spirited, hard to please and self-important.

No contest.

She looked back at Lance and Marissa, heads bent together earnestly, one dark, one light, and realized maybe there were things poor little rich kids had to complain about. It was an unexpectedly freeing thought.

But as she gazed at the two heads, she felt a little lonely. Left out. That was the hard part of never having enough; you always felt like the world was inside a big, cheery room, while you stood on the outside in the cold, looking through the windows.

As she was looking at Lance now. Even though she'd made up her mind to avoid him, it was painful to have him here, so close and yet so unavailable.

Live with it, she told herself. Even if he'd never met her cousin, if he'd never crossed her path in any way, Lance Forrest was not the kind of man she wanted to waste her time with.

She'd just put him out of her mind.

Chapter Seven

As the evening wore on, however, Tamara could not completely ignore him. It was impossible, like trying to ignore the honeyed sunshine pouring from a balloon-colored summer sky.

And hard as she tried not to do it, she found herself wondering what had made Lance ask Marissa to dance in the first place. Had he felt sorry for her? Had it been some twisted way of showing just how desirable he was?

He was obviously having a good time with her. They laughed and made jokes. Once Lance literally threw his head back and guffawed at something she said. A bright light shone in Marissa's eyes then, giving Tamara a deep, wrenching twist in her gut.

Tamara scowled. She didn't believe Lance would really date a girl like this. She doubted any man with an ego like his would. They picked women for the way they looked—the best of the best, not even a little bit flawed, and God forbid any should be that great American horror: overweight!

Was Lance simply being kind? If that were the case, it worried her. Marissa might take things the wrong way and get her heart broken.

Washing glasses at the sink, Tamara overheard Lance say, "Too bad you're too young for me. You really make me laugh."

Marissa smiled saucily. "Maybe you aren't my type, sweetheart."

"I'm crushed." Lance flirted back.

When Marissa's friends gathered her up, it was almost closing time. Marissa hurriedly scribbled her name and number on a napkin. "Tamara," she called. "I really meant it about accounting. If you have trouble, call me."

"Oh, you'll give her your number, but not me, huh?" Lance said, plucking up the napkin. "You don't mind if I copy it down first, do you, Tamara?"

Judging by the tight knot in her chest, Tamara did mind. "Why would I care? It's Marissa you should be asking."

Ignoring her, Lance took out a little black book—now why wasn't she surprised that he should have one?—and scribbled the number down. "I'm serious about the melodrama," he said to Marissa. "Call me when it comes up."

"I will." She patted his shoulder and waved gaily at Tamara.

Lance handed the napkin to Tamara. "If you flunked that test, you really might give her a call."

Tamara nodded and tucked the note in her pocket. The bar was clearing now. "It's fifteen minutes to last call," she said in a businesslike voice. "Do you want another beer?"

He pursed his lips and tilted the bottle. The expression made his mouth look infinitely devourable, and a bolt of something hot and needy pulsed through her unexpectedly. "I'm gonna have to walk home either way, so yeah," he said, "give me one more."

He stood up to pull money from the front pocket of his jeans, and Tamara found her gaze caressing his strong thighs and the weighty place between—

She jerked her gaze away, a painful shame burning to the tips of her ears. Ducking, she fished out another bottle of beer and put it on the counter and took the bills he'd put down without looking at him. She made change and put it on the bar.

"Do you have a favorite song?" he asked, taking quarters from the change.

"Pardon me?"

"A favorite song. Do you have something you like on the jukebox? I thought I'd play some mellow stuff to get everybody tired so you can go home." His dimpled grin flashed.

In every millimeter of her body, Tamara flushed in response. Damn him. It was not fair he should be so irresistible, that he should appear when she was feeling so vulnerable. With a frown, she shook her head. "I've heard them all so many times, it doesn't matter."

"C'mon," he coaxed. "There must be one you like."

Her tangled, roused emotions suddenly swelled.

"Will you stop being so charming? I don't need your pity. Neither does Marissa, for that matter."

"Pity?" He repeated the word quietly.

"Yeah. Is this your charity week?" she said, heedless now. She saw the slight narrowing of his eyes and it goaded her further. "You think I don't know you would never date a woman like that? Do you think she doesn't know it? I think it's cruel to lead someone on."

"Is that what you think?" He was very still.

"Yes."

Very slowly, he stood up and gathered his change, down to the last dime. His face had none of the boyish charm to it now, only a grim tightness around the beautiful mouth. "You don't get it, Tamara." He shook his head. "Not everybody has an ulterior motive all the time. Sometimes it's good to just enjoy the moment. Besides," he said, disdainfully tossing a dollar bill for a tip down on the bar, "who is doing the judging here, anyway? Are you the one who picks out the girls who get to have boyfriends and which ones sit on the sidelines?"

Instantly, Tamara was ashamed. What she'd been feeling was pure, uncut jealousy, and it had made her catty.

But before she could form an apology, Lance was gone, his beer left untouched on the bar. He yanked the door open with enough force that she knew she'd made him angry, and for some reason, it made her heart ache.

Resolutely, she started breaking down the bar. It was better this way. Maybe he'd leave her alone now and she could get on with her life without wondering every minute if Lance Forrest was going to grace her with a smile.

Lance strode through the chilly night for two blocks before reason penetrated the faintly inebriated haze that colored his feelings. Damn the woman, anyway. Who did she think she was, making judgments like that?

All evening, he'd done his best to show her he wasn't the cad she thought he was. Halfway through his conversation with Alonzo, he'd remembered how easy it had been to be with her at her house, when he was too tired to turn on the charm and try to impress her. And it had annoyed him. Instead of mooning over her, he'd decided to follow Jake's example and try to have a good time. Marissa had proved to be a terrific companion, easy going and happy to playfully flirt. He wasn't quite sure why he'd sat at the bar....

That was a lie. He'd wanted to be close to Tamara. But all it had done was make her mad.

Or jealous.

He slowed. Stopped. Turned around to glance back at the neon sign that blinked against the backdrop of black mountain. "Well, I'll be damned," he said aloud.

Had that been jealousy on her face when she snatched the phone number from his hand? He turned his mind back over the signals she'd put out while he sat and talked with Marissa. Slamming glasses. Rattling ice. Restlessly moving back and forth between one end of the bar and the other.

He grinned, and started walking back to the bar. Jealous he knew how to handle.

The parking lot was fairly well cleared out by the time he got back there. A waitress waved at him wearily and he lifted his chin, taking up his spot to wait for Tamara—leaning against the hood of her Buick.

He didn't have long to wait. She came out minutes later, pulling the pins out of her hair, probably in protection against the cold. It tumbled in a glossy swath to her shoulders. She gave a little shake of her head and rolled her neck.

And then she saw him, leaning against her car under the streetlight, his arms crossed. She stopped dead, and Lance knew that if there had been any other option besides coming toward him, she'd have taken it.

Her pointed little chin jutted up, and she hauled her bag close to her side, as if she were preparing for battle. As she came closer, he let himself simply look at her, as he'd been longing to do all night. He watched her dark hair swing, catching the light from the red neon behind her. He admired the long legs and the easy way she moved.

"Do you need a ride?" she asked, fitting her key into the door lock.

He had to hand it to her, she was cool as the night. He shook his head.

She opened the door, hesitated. "I'm sorry about what I said in the bar," she said.

Lance nodded, and didn't move.

"You're on my car. I can't go until you move."

"I know." He lazily stood up and moved toward her. In her eyes he saw a faint flare of alarm and desire. He didn't smile this time. "I don't really want you to go just yet."

As Lance came toward her, Tamara shrank into the

space between the open door and the car, her fingers clutched tight around the top of the window. Only when he moved in close did she realize she'd been neatly trapped. She ducked her head, as if he might go away if she didn't look at him.

"Come here, sugar," he said, and reached out to put a hand on her waist, sliding it under her jacket where it was warm. With a quick gesture, he found the belt loop on the side of her jeans and laced two fingers through it. With a steady pull, he pulled her close, but not quite in contact with him.

"Lance!" she protested, putting her hands up to push him away. "You're just mad at me—"

"Not at all." He found himself tasting his lips, remembering the flavor of her there, on his mouth. "I think I just want to kiss you."

"I wish you'd stop teasing me," she said, squirming a little. She still didn't look at him.

"Teasing? Is that what I'm doing?" Something thick settled over him, her nearness, something heavy and narcotic that blunted any sense or reason he might have had at the beginning. There was only Tamara, smelling faintly of shampoo and hard work and something sweet he couldn't quite place. "No," he said quietly, "I don't think I'm teasing."

He slid his other hand around her, and spread both hands open on her back. She came up against him, breasts to chest, thighs to thighs, and he heard a quick intake of breath catch in her throat, but she didn't push away. Not this time.

"You feel nice," he said, moving his hands lightly. "This is what I've been thinking of all night, Tamara, you know that? Thinking about how I could get your body next to mine, so I could feel you." Her back was long and curved and the flesh quivered ever so slightly as he caressed it, but there was resistance all through her.

She tilted her face up. In her eyes shone fear and desire and hunger, all tangled. Her hands had stopped pushing his chest, and he felt her breath come quicker, lifting her breasts into his rib cage at heady little intervals.

The thick sense of narcotic pleasure grew, and he let his gaze drop down to her mouth, the mouth he'd been imagining all night long, the mouth that had tasted so sweet the other night. Letting his anticipation build, he looked at the small bow on the upper lip, and the plump lower lip that jutted out ever so slightly, and let desire fill his every cell, relishing the building anticipation until it made him dizzy.

When he could no longer bear the sight of those slightly parted lips only inches from his own, when the wish for her mouth against his was larger than the sky overhead, only then did he bend his head. Tilt his mouth. Pause, millimeters away, to let the prickles of need cover his skin while cool air mingled with the heat of their intertwined breath.

His heart thudded in his chest in that split second. Thick washes of blood moved in his veins. He felt her thighs against his own, and the uplifted softness of her breasts and the fine quiver of muscles in her back. It was heady, rich, unbearable.

With an outcast breath, he closed the space between them, settled his lips upon hers. Once again, it was a vivid shock, too big for a kiss.

This time, she made a faint sound and lifted her

arms around his neck, pulling him closer. Lance reacted violently, mindlessly. He yanked her hard against him, hips to hips, backed her against the car and kissed her. This time it wasn't soft or restrained. This time, she opened her mouth, inviting him into the dark cavern, and Lance plunged in, knowing he was lost as soon as he did it. She clutched his head, pulling him closer, and he pressed his whole self into her.

The narcotic pleasure swirled and pulsed and intensified until Lance thought of nothing, past or present, but the taste of her mouth fitting so perfectly with his own. Under his hands, her body softened, and she wriggled closer, making him ache. He explored the parts of her mouth he'd been thinking of and the parts he had not thought to consider. He let his tongue dance with hers, and flitter and plunge, and she met him with exquisite timing, as if she knew what he would do, what he thought, before he did.

He slipped his hands under her shirt in the back and touched the heat of her bare skin. She shuddered, pausing a moment as if the sensation were too rich to encompass without perfect attention.

And then he realized he was extremely aroused. Furiously so. He nipped at her lip a little and she only tightened her fingers against his scalp. He pressed his arousal into the softness of her belly and she only moved restless against him.

He broke away from her lips and buried his face in her neck. Such soft, soft skin. Softer than fur, softer than talcum powder, softer than anything he'd ever touched. In fierce desire, he let his hands fall and curl around her buttocks, firm and full. He sucked lightly at her neck, loving the sound of surprised, sharp pleasure she made, and the way she shivered against him. He kissed her throat.

"Oh, sugar," he breathed. "I can't remember when I wanted a woman this bad." He heard the need rasping his voice, and didn't care. "Let me take you home."

Let me take you home.

The words penetrated the haze over Tamara with a cruel, piercing shock. She froze against him, fighting the glorious sensation of his lips moving over her throat, over her chin. "No," she whispered. "Lance, no, I—"

His mouth claimed hers once more. Rich lips, full and firm and exquisitely mobile, and so very, very hungry. It was that yearning tenderness that undid her. Expertise or passion would not have surprised her, or unnerved her.

This sweetness did. The way he pulled her close against him suggestively, but cradled her body as if it were fragile and precious. The way he trembled faintly. The way he kissed her.

And he felt so good. His broad hands. His mouth. The solid mass of his shoulders and his taut back and hard thighs. That solidness felt shielding and safe and she wanted never to let him go. Under her hands, his neck was hot and his hair was cool, and he made a deep, throaty noise of longing that went straight to the core of her abdomen.

It had been so long. So long. Kissing Lance after a long day, she wanted only to be naked with him, to take the pleasure he offered so freely, and to give him rest and peace in return. Maybe if he were safely buried between her thighs, he could forget what haunted him, what made him seem so lost, what made him—

She pushed against him. "Lance, no! This is crazy," she whispered. She shifted away, pushing a little at his shoulders. He moved his hands back to her waist and lifted his head.

His eyes, sober and dark and hazed with desire, made her hips soften all over again. "It's supposed to be crazy," he said and touched her lower lip with just the tip of his tongue.

Tamara shuddered. She ducked her head suddenly. "I can't do this. I can't. I'm not like you."

Somewhere behind him, a door slammed, and he shifted quickly, smoothing her clothes. He captured one of her hands and planted a kiss to her palm. "No, you aren't. Like me."

For some reason, that tenderness made her want to weep. Made her want to give him anything he wanted, anything he asked, just so she could make his way easier for an hour or a day, or whatever he'd let her offer.

"Look at me, Tamara," he said.

Struggling with the unexpectedly fierce longing, Tamara didn't move.

"It's only a good-night kiss," he said, putting his hand under her chin to raise her face. She allowed it, but did not raise her eyes.

He put his mouth on hers. Gently. So gently. "Good night," he said, and let her go. Without looking back, he loped off into the darkness.

Tamara watched him go with a sinking heart. He moved like a stag, wild and free, his hair shining faintly in the lights of buildings along the way. A wild creature.

And she was not wild or free. She was captured. Trapped. And the one time she'd dared to ask anything for herself, for something bigger than what life had seen fit to provide, she'd been tied and gagged so tightly, she still had trouble breathing.

Not because of Cody—she could never regret that he was part of her life. But she would so love to travel with him, to give him a better life, to give him chances it would be very difficult to provide for him now.

Lance could provide them.

The thought stole in traitorously. Lance could give Cody things—education and opportunities and experiences Tamara never could. He was low-key about it, but she knew he was very wealthy, and not only by virtue of inheriting controlling interest in Forrest Construction, which had made a fortune on the upscale houses in the area, but on his own. Word was he'd sold his half of the business in Houston for a very pretty penny.

Wearily, she got in her car and started it up. It rumbled to life instantly, and she pulled out, her thoughts troubled.

Thinking of Lance as a money cow was wrong. If she wanted to let him know he had a son, and let him do what he thought was right, she had to do it for the right reasons.

There was only one right reason, only one good reason: because he had a right to know he had a child in the world. Because Cody had a right to know his father.

But would Lance be any kind of father? Could a

creature that wild and free give anything to a woman or a child except momentary pleasure, fleeting joy?

Half an hour later, after picking Cody up from his baby-sitter's house, Tamara still didn't have the answer to that question. As she carried the sleeping boy to his bed, the only thing she understood clearly was that Lance Forrest, kissing her with such hungry vulnerability, was not the same man she had believed he was all these years.

And she had to find out who he was before anything else could be solved. Before she could trust him with the knowledge of his child.

But that meant allowing herself to be in his company, and even more, forcing herself to try to be objective. It would mean that at some moment, he would kiss her again like he had tonight. And meant she might not resist his invitation to his bed the next time.

Could she bear it? How could she stand to let that wanting grow? Risk wanting anything, ever again?

In his bed, Cody sleepily turned over, and she tucked his covers over his slim shoulder. Light fell from the hallway over his small, still face, and Tamara saw his father in the clean carved lines, saw where the baby plumpness would one day whittle down and where a beard would grow. In the silky tresses, she felt the thickness that it would take on. Like his father's.

Tenderly she kissed him. For Cody she could do anything.

Anything.

Chapter Eight

Lance rose early Saturday. He felt muddled and off center, not quite like himself. It didn't feel like too much drink, but he couldn't quite place the feeling, either. As he shaved, he wondered wryly if it were Tamara, if she were a drug he ought to stay away from.

Viewed in the bright light of morning, his reaction to kissing her seemed absurd. He rinsed his razor and frowned, remembering that weird, lost, unthinking haze that had come over him. He liked kissing, and he liked Tamara, but last night had just been—

Well...*weird.* That was the only word he could think of.

But he didn't have time to dwell on it this morning. He had to go scour Red Creek for rentals. Last night, Lance had discovered that Alonzo was living in a motel. Thanks to the ski slopes within easy driving distance and the almost insane upswing of the economy lately, rents were outrageous—not easily in the reach of even a well-paid construction worker.

Lance washed shaving cream from his face. His help this morning wasn't unselfish by any stretch. Lance had worked with adobe makers in Houston and San Antonio, and none of them had come close to the exquisite work Alonzo could do. In addition, Alonzo had the rare ability to teach his craft to others, and run a crew reliably and with good humor.

Lance didn't want to lose him.

Unfortunately, a dozen calls, and even the yanking of a few strings, turned up nothing. With the first snows around the corner, all the rentals in the area were locked up tight. Lance found one available property—a luxury home a half hour away that rented for three times what Alonzo made in a month.

Finally, driven by desperation, Lance called his mother to ask about the guest house that sat on their land. She hesitated for one long moment, and then said, "Let me meet him first."

So Lance picked up Alonzo with the vague promise that they'd look at rentals after a while, but he wanted to go by and see his mother first.

Louise answered the door, wearing an apron over her plump curves. Flour dusted her. "Y'all come on in. I have to get these muffins out of the oven. My timer just went off." Leaving the door open, she hurried off.

"Oh, you're in for a treat," Lance said with a grin. "She's one of the best cooks in the state."

"Yeah?" A curious expression, half amused, half surprised, was on Alonzo's face. "I miss good food."

"Don't tell her. She'll have you fat as a hog in two weeks flat." He gestured for Alonzo to enter. "My mother loves to cook—but even more, she likes to feed people."

Alonzo smoothed his mustache, raising one devilish black eyebrow. "An old-fashioned woman." He winked. "I like that. You young ones, you don't know yet what's important in a woman."

Lance thought of Tamara. For a fleeting second, he tasted her lips on his own. Then his mind snagged on the way her house had seemed so warm and comfortable and easy to be in, the night of his father's funeral. He remembered awakening, fed and soothed, in her chair, covered by a blanket she had placed over him.

The memory gave him a strange twist in his gut. He frowned. "You might be surprised," he said to Alonzo.

They followed Louise to the kitchen, where she was taking out a tray of enormous, steaming blueberry muffins. Lance's mouth watered instantly. "Those look good. Don't tell me you're making them for some museum tea or something."

"No sir, they are not." She gave him her sunniest smile. "I made them for you and your friend." Putting the tray on top of the stove, she took off her oven mitt and held out a hand to Alonzo. "You must be Alonzo Chacon. I'm Louise Forrest. My boy has been singin' your praises for weeks now. I'm glad to meet you."

Alonzo moved forward, and took the outstretched hand. With a courtly gesture, he bent over it and planted a kiss lightly to the knuckles. "They did not tell me you were so beautiful," he said.

"Flattery will get you everywhere, Mr. Chacon," she said briskly, taking back her hand.

"No flattery," Alonzo said, inclining his head with a smile. He touched his hand to his chest. "From the heart."

To Lance's amazement, his mother blushed faintly, the color washing over the clear, smooth cheeks in a way he found touching. "Y'all sit down in the dining room and I'll bring the muffins. Lance, you grab the butter. The real butter, now."

"I know, Mom." She didn't allow margarine to taint her bakery goods.

He carried the ceramic butter dish to the table. "Why do we get blueberry muffins? What's the occasion?"

"No occasion," she said airily, and Lance knew something was up. "I was hoping you might be able to help me with an errand this afternoon. The new museum curator is coming in today, and I want to be there to go over things with her."

Lance buttered a muffin, waiting for the other shoe. "But—?" he prompted.

"Well, I promised Mrs. Jordan I'd help her with her shopping. You know she can't drive anymore, not since that little accident last summer—"

"Little accident, my eye." Lance snorted. "She took out three parking meters and the front window of a dry cleaner's shop."

Alonzo's eye twinkled, but he was absorbed in his muffin.

"Anyway," Louise continued, "she needs to go to

the grocery store. I know she's fussy, but you're so patient with her, and I was hoping you might do it in my place."

Lance shrugged. "Okay."

Louise reached over and patted his arm. "You're such a good boy. What would I do without you?" She looked at Alonzo. "You know, when he was a child, I could always count on Lance to run any errand I needed, even when he had to ride his bike all the way down the hill."

"Down was never the trouble. *Up* was the killer."

Alonzo neatly blotted his mustache. "Delicious!" he pronounced. "I eat too much food from restaurants. And food needs a woman's hand, you know?"

"Are you always so charming, Mr. Chacon?"

He winked. "Yes."

Louise chuckled and pushed the basket closer to him. "Well, it's always a pleasure to feed a man who appreciates it. Help yourself."

Happily, Alonzo picked out another muffin. *"Gracias."*

While getting dressed Saturday morning, Tamara was appalled to find she had a hickey on her neck. A hickey! Leaning into the mirror, she touched the red mark with embarrassment and a certain heat. She hadn't even noticed that Lance had been nibbling that hard.

Her skin showed bruises easily. Maybe he'd only been—

She sank down to the bed, her hand over the bruise, suddenly awash in sensual memories. His mouth, moving over her neck, supping at her flesh as if he were starving. His hands down her back, on her bottom, against her ear.

She closed her eyes. She was in so far over her head! Lance Forrest was out of her league on every imaginable level. He was gorgeous and rich and experienced. What in the world did he even find to like about her?

With a sigh, she dug through her drawers, looking for something that might be used to cover up the mark. All she could find was a soft cotton turtleneck that was a bit too warm for the weather. It was fall, but the day was bright and sunny. In the mountains, Indian summer might mean anything from fifty to eighty degrees.

"Mommy!" Cody said from the doorway. "Are we ever going to go?" Saturdays were the only days Tamara had to spend long hours with her son. She combined trips to the park or the hills with whatever small errands she needed to run. They often stopped to have a cup of chocolate at the diner when they were finished, and Cody loved it. He looked forward to Saturdays all week long.

"I'm almost done, honey. Watch the rest of your show, and I'll be ready."

"Hurry, okay?"

Tamara kissed his blond head. "I will, sweetie."

He ambled off, and Tamara tossed on the turtleneck with a pair of jeans, and hurried through her makeup. It was only as she caught sight of herself in the mirror in the living room that she remembered why she wore this shirt with something over it. She stopped, frowning. It wasn't particularly tight, or revealing—after all, how revealing could a long-sleeved turtleneck be?—

but it always seemed to do something wild to her figure. The soft fabric clung lightly to her every curve, and the color was vivid.

"You look really nice, Mommy," Cody said. He lifted a hand and rubbed her arm.

Tamara smiled at him. "Thanks." What was she so afraid of, anyway? Wasn't she just whining to herself last night about wanting to look good?

Yeah, but that was before Lance had kissed her. Before he brought alive every sexual longing she'd ever even thought about having.

Oh, honestly! she thought with exasperation. She had to stop this. With a wry grin at Cody, she said, "C'mon, kiddo, let's go have some fun."

Cody played in the park, on the swings and merry-go-round and the slides, tumbling and running and hollering. Afterward, they had their cocoa at the B & B Café.

And all day, men flirted with Tamara. At first, it puzzled her. It wasn't something that happened to her very often. Never had. Valerie always told her she put out touch-me-not signals.

As the day wore on, Tamara wondered in some confusion if Lance had found the "on" button. Something had certainly changed. The old man at the gas station, who never wore his teeth and shaved maybe every third day, gave her a gummy smile and a wink with her change. A biker guy in the park, who might have looked dangerous in his leathers and long hair without the bevy of toddlers he rolled with in the grass, smiled at her every time she happened to glance his way.

Even a young man, barely out of his teens, looked over his shoulder as he walked by.

Must be the turtleneck, Tamara thought.

Their last stop for the day was at the supermarket for coffee. She ordinarily avoided Saturdays at the market, but there were things in life she wouldn't do without.

As she turned the corner, Cody spied the carnival. "Oh, Mommy, look!" he said in the voice of awe reserved for children under five, and fourteen-year-olds in love. "A carnibal! Can we go?"

Tamara eyed the Ferris wheel and tented booths set up in the vacant lot beyond the grocery store, wondering how she'd missed its arrival. "I don't know, Cody." She did a few quick calculations, wondering if she dared take some of the tips from her earnings last night to do this for him. She had one week to gather the funds for the phone bill, or they'd cut her phone off.

But she did have a week and she worked every day between now and then. Even if she did lose the phone, it didn't matter much. No one much ever called her.

"Pretty please with sugar on top?" Cody wheedled. He knew he'd won, and the bright blue eyes twinkled in his cherubic face. Tamara suddenly saw Lance in that twinkle, and wondered if he had been this adorable as a child.

"We'll go," she said. "But first you have to go home and take a nap. It's more fun at night, when all the lights are on, and everything looks pretty."

"Yippee! And we can get cotton candy!"

She patted his knee. "Yep, cotton candy. Pink for me."

"Blue for me!"

"You've got it, kiddo." She spied an empty parking space in the crowded lot. "Let's go get my coffee and get you home for a nap, and after supper we'll go to the carnival."

As they entered the busy store, Tamara was caught suddenly by the strangeness of the place again. While she'd been growing up, Red Creek had been a sleepy, nowhere little town on the way to the ski resorts. This market had then been ten aisles wide, with maybe two variations of brands available, and the customers had been ranchers in pickup trucks, and plain-speaking natives in sensible clothes. Once in a while, a glamorous type from Denver or Aspen were forced to spend the night at the Sleepy Owl Motel, but they cleared out as soon as possible.

The wild expansion of the last few years had begun while Tamara was away at college, and the changes it had wrought still occasionally took her by surprise. The market was truly a supermarket these days, with twenty five aisles of high-gloss floors. The customers were young, or trying to remain so as long as possible, and took fitness very seriously in their newfound home. L.L. Bean clothes abounded. The ranchers, in their worn boots and Western-cut jeans and broken-in hats, looked as out of place as a coal stove in a gourmet kitchen.

But there wasn't any other place to shop. And thanks to the rocketing rise of land prices, some of those laid-back ranchers were pretty well-off themselves.

Tamara liked some of it. In the coffee aisle, she could choose from scores of brands, packaged or loose, whole bean or ground. The produce aisle groaned with exotic offerings of every imaginable variety, and the magazine aisle carried everything from confessions to Martha Stewart.

Still it dazzled her at times. Today she didn't feel as uncomfortable as she sometimes did, and she cheerfully swung Cody's hand next to her, ambling through and watching people covertly. She took Cody to the coloring books and let him pick through them, all the while covertly admiring a woman in her late forties who wore black leggings and had the rear end of a sixteen-year-old.

A voice said playfully in her ear, "She's not your type, I'm afraid."

Lance. Tamara looked up, fighting the rush of welcome and heat she felt at the sound of his voice in her ear. He looked as touchable as always, blond and clean and gleaming, with just enough of a rakish air to be interesting. "I was just wondering," Tamara said, "what she has to do to keep looking like that."

He inclined his head, admiring the woman's long legs and firm bottom. A slow grin crossed his face and he gave Tamara a wicked look, raising one approving eyebrow. "Whatever it is," he said, "it's worth it."

Tamara chuckled. It was hard to argue with that logic.

An elderly woman with her glasses on a chain over her blue cardigan thrust a handful of coupons into Lance's hands. "I don't have time for all your flirtin' today, boy." She poked a bony finger at the top coupon. "See if you can find that brand for me. I'll swear, these glasses still aren't right."

Lance shot Tamara a bright glance from the corner

of his eye. "Mrs. Jordan, this is Tamara Flynn. She's a friend of mine."

"How do you do, young lady," the woman said, looking over her glasses. "Is that your boy there?"

Tamara nodded. "This is Cody. Cody, say hello to Mrs. Jordan."

Cody looked up. "Hi." Caught by something on her sweater, he leaned closer. "Cool pin!"

"It's a poison pin!" She exclaimed, and bent over to show Cody the antique pin with its empty container.

Tamara stood there in the florescent-lit aisle, trying to pretend she didn't notice Lance's shirt was open to the third button. She tried not to notice how alluring she found the tendons of his neck when he turned his head, or that he smelled of something spicy. She tried to pretend her gaze didn't skitter over his smiling mouth every ten seconds and fall on his hands, so broad and strong, the rest of the time.

She really tried not to notice the way he was looking at her, a little shyly, when he thought she wouldn't notice, or that his gaze traveled all over her.

But both of them looked up at the same instant. Tamara was swept into the bright jeweled blue, snagged hard on the half-sober, half-teasing way he looked at her. She couldn't think of anything to say, and she couldn't look away, and so they just stood there looking at each other for a long time. Tamara wondered if he was remembering the kiss last night, as she was—

He touched her hand with his index finger. Covertly, so only she would know. "Would you let me take you and Cody to the carnival tonight?"

The words didn't penetrate for a minute. "The carnival?" she echoed.

His grin flashed then, that irascible, devil-may-care grin that went straight through her. "You know, the one right outside here? I figured it might be something you could do with your son, so you wouldn't have to find a baby-sitter."

Damn him. For an irresponsible wild man, he was awfully considerate sometimes. Or was that good? Tamara couldn't remember. He also made it very hard to think rationally.

"That would be great," Tamara heard herself say. "I can't stay out late, though."

"That's fine. How about if I come get you around six?"

"Make it seven, so I can feed him before we go."

He shook his head. "I'll buy you both supper."

"Me?" Cody said, having learned everything he could from Mrs. Jordan about her pin. "Can I have one of them big hot dogs?"

"'May I,'" Tamara said automatically. "And 'one of those,' not 'them.'"

Cody rolled his eyes, and Lance ruffled his hair in the classic male gesture of affection. "Listen to your mom. And yes, you *may* have one of *those* hot dogs."

Mrs. Jordan poked Lance's arm. "Enough, young man. I don't have all day."

"Yes, ma'am," Lance said, and moved off, allowing Mrs. Jordan to lean on him as they went down the aisle.

Tamara watched them go, struck by the rarity of a man that patient. Maybe she'd been wrong about him. It sure looked that way.

Then Mrs. Jordan glanced over her shoulder, and there was no mistaking the expression on her wizened face.

Pity.

Tamara blushed. Even old Mrs. Jordan knew Lance's reputation as a ladies' man—and she thought Tamara was his next victim.

Tamara lifted her chin. Mrs. Jordan didn't know anything.

Chapter Nine

Louise Forrest loved carnivals, always had. She liked the smell of them—cotton candy and dust and frying onions. She liked the tubes of neon in candy colors and the tinny music and the crowds of people. Most of all, she loved the feverishness of the combination, the excitement.

Tonight was no different. She and her youngest son, Tyler, had brought Curtis out to ride the kiddie rides. They stood by the baby Ferris wheel, waving at the three-year-old cheerfully when Louise caught sight of Lance and a woman coming closer.

Louise grabbed Tyler's arm. "Who's the woman your brother is with?"

"I knew he wasn't going to leave her alone." His mouth thinned. "That's Tamara Flynn. She's a bartender at the Wild Moose."

"Is that her child?"

"Yeah." Ty gave his mother an odd look. "Why?"

Louise pursed her lips and looked at Curtis, who was now free of the Ferris wheel and bolted toward them, blond hair flying, face full of glee. Then she looked at the boy walking alongside Lance, bubbling about something.

No, she wasn't mistaken.

The boys could be twins.

Louise raised her gaze to the dark-haired woman's face, and in a fleeting instant before the girl covered her expression, there was pure, terrified panic.

Faintly, Louise smiled. Interesting. Very interesting indeed.

Until the moment they encountered Lance's mother and brother, Tamara had been enjoying herself immensely. Cody was rested from a long nap, and the night was comfortable. Walking next to Lance, holding Cody's hand, Tamara felt young for the first time in years. Young and carefree.

It was heavenly.

Until they ran into Louise Forrest at the kiddie Ferris wheel, and one of Tamara's most dreaded moments came to pass.

It was impossible to miss the resemblance between Cody and Curtis—and Tamara had always thought it odd that their names were so similar, too. She had seen Tyler and his son when the boys were one and two, respectively, and had known to stay clear of all Forrests thereafter. It wasn't completely possible—she knew Curtis sometimes went to Cody's day care, for example—but she did her best.

It wasn't strange to her that neither Lance nor Tyler had noticed the resemblance between the boys. Men just didn't notice such things unless a woman brought it to their attention.

Louise was the one Tamara worried about. A man might be oblivious, but never a mother, and never, ever a grandmother. And judging by the measuring expression on her face, Louise didn't need anyone to point out anything.

Since Tamara couldn't very well grab Cody and bolt now, she moved forward on leaden legs, trying to keep her face expressionless and distantly friendly.

"Uncle Lanth!" Curtis cried, and rushed into his arms. "I rode the Ferrith wheel!"

Lance picked him up easily, and Tamara felt a queer little flip in her stomach. He had such a sweet way with children. It lulled her into thinking he was steady. That would be a mistake. Gentle didn't necessarily mean reliable.

"You did?" Lance said. "Do you want to go again, with Cody? It might be more fun for both of you to have somebody to ride with."

"Yeah, I do," Curtis said, peeking over Lance's shoulder at Cody.

"Cool!" Cody cried. "Can I?"

Tamara nodded. Her heart raced, but she tried to act normally. "Sure."

"Mama," Lance said, "this is Tamara Flynn. My mother, Louise Forrest."

"Hello," Tamara said, quietly.

"Nice to meet you, Tamara," Louise replied. Her bright blue eyes were the exact same shade as Lance and Cody's, and Tamara felt a pang of conscience.

Whatever her reservations about Lance as a father figure, Tamara had also deprived a grandmother of her grandchild.

She looked away, glad of the distraction when the boys climbed into the car of the Ferris wheel. She gave the man tending the ride some tickets.

Lance bent over the boys, making sure they were securely fastened before he let the attendant close the safety cage. Looking at the pair of preschoolers side by side, Tamara was amazed how very much alike they looked. It was more than similar coloring and bone structure; they had mirroring gestures and facial expressions, as well.

Tamara crossed her arms. Considering they lived in the same small town, it was amazing that someone had not commented on it before now.

Or maybe it wasn't. Maybe a lot more people knew the truth than didn't. In that case, it might be considered bad manners to comment.

"Why, those two boys could be kin!" Louise exclaimed.

"I never noticed how much Cody looks like Curtis," Lance said, almost at the same moment.

Tamara tried to take a breath no one would notice. She let it out slowly, and murmured, "Mmm-hmm."

"It's amazing," Lance said.

The only one who'd said nothing was Tyler, and Tamara felt his silence like a siren. He stood next to her, quiet, and she snuck a glance at him. He seemed to sense her gaze, and looked down.

He winked.

It was the first time Tamara had ever seen anything

like amusement or anything half resembling a smile on his face.

He knew.

Of course he did. His late wife had worked with Valerie for a while. He would know the whole story. The *whole* story.

She smiled in thanks. She didn't know why, but her gut told her she could trust the silent, haunted mountain man.

"Oh, look what a nice time they're having together!" Louise exclaimed. "How about letting us take Cody with us, and you two can go and have a beer or something?"

Tamara looked at Lance. Something hot and wicked rose in his eyes, and she suddenly wanted very much to have the chance to be alone with him for a little while. Just to talk. Hold hands, maybe. Listen to him laugh.

Touch him. The very strength of the longing made her protest. "I don't know how Cody will feel about that."

"Let's ask him," Tyler said. "Curtis doesn't get to be around other children much, since we live so far out, but Cody probably does. He might want to be with his mom."

As the boys came off the Ferris wheel, Curtis loped along beside Cody, his cowboy boots scuffing up dust. Hesitantly, Curtis reached for Cody's hand.

Cody looked a little surprised, but he didn't pull away. In fact, he leaned close, in a protective, older brother kind of way, and said, "Were you scared?"

Curtis made a guileless face. "Juth a little bit."

Louise chuckled, and put a hand on Lance's shoulder. "You were just like that with Jake. Worshiped the ground he walked upon."

"C'mon, Ma," Lance said with a chuckle. "Don't embarrass me in front of my girl, now."

His girl. The phrase felt insulting and warming all at once. "I'm no girl, Mr. Forrest, and I don't belong to anyone."

"Here, here," Tyler said.

"Mommy," Cody said. "Can I ride with Curtis on all the rides? I think he needs somebody bigger."

Tamara smiled. "Sure. Come here and let me ask you something."

"I'll be right back," Cody said.

When they were out of earshot of the others, Tamara said, "Curtis's grandma and daddy are going to take him to all the kid rides. Do you feel okay going with them? I'm just thinking about riding the big Ferris wheel with Mr. Forrest."

"Sure! I like Curtis's daddy. He brings me gum."

"Oh, he does? I didn't know that."

Cody gave her a patient sigh. "Curtis and me eat lunch together whenever he comes to school." His eyes narrowed faintly. "Curtis has a Power Rangers lunch box. And his dad makes him beef jerky instead of peanut butter."

"Is that right," Tamara said dryly. She stood and took his hand. "If you don't mind, then, I will go ride the grown-up rides."

"With Mr. Forrest #1," he said with a bubble of laughter. "I'm going with Mr. Forrest #2."

"And Mrs. Forrest," she said as they rejoined the others.

"Oh, heck, you can call me 'Grandma,'" Louise

said with a wink. "Everybody else does." She looked at Tamara. "That is if you don't mind."

Tamara couldn't help it. Under the bright pointedness of Louise's gaze, she blushed. "I don't mind," she said quietly.

Louise smiled. "All right, then, boys," she said, taking a hand of each, "let's go have us a time!"

"See you after a while," Ty said. "But don't hold your breath. You know how Mama is about carnivals."

"I remember," Lance said. "Thanks, man."

"No problem. Curtis will love it." Ty gave Tamara a faint smile. "All I ever hear about after a day at preschool is Cody this, Cody that. Cody knows how to read. Cody has a Batman lunch box."

Tamara chuckled. "And Cody just told me that Curtis has Power Rangers."

"Maybe they should trade," Lance said, taking her hand. He waved the other at Ty pointedly. "Bye now."

Tamara looked up at Lance in surprise. If any other man had behaved this way, she would have sworn he was jealous. But Lance? He didn't strike her as a particularly jealous type.

Ty leaned over and said something in Lance's ear. An odd, hard expression crossed Lance's face as Ty straightened. "Don't take him too seriously," Ty said to Tamara, and walked away before she could reply.

"I think you have a fan," Lance said. His voice sounded tight. "I haven't heard him say three words to a woman since his wife died."

Tamara looked at him, lacing her fingers more closely around his, liking the strength and power in them. "You know," she said with a smile, "you almost sound jealous."

"You know what?" he said, leaning close, "I think I am." His expression showed puzzlement. "That's not usually my style."

She didn't know what to say to that, but it gave her a quick, hopeful rush. Standing there in the unseasonably warm night, with wild colors staining the air, Tamara simply looked at him. "You keep surprising me," she said at last.

"Yeah?" he said. "Does that mean you aren't going to be mean to me anymore?"

Tamara laughed. "I don't know. Depends on how well you mind your manners."

He lifted a wicked brow. "Ah, you wouldn't make me behave, would you? I'm so much better bad."

She rolled her eyes. "Full of bad clichés, you mean."

"Maybe." He grinned and tugged her hand. "Let's go find us some wild rides," he said, and wiggled that wicked brow one more time.

In spite of herself, Tamara laughed, and let him lead her away.

Lance had not had so much fun in years. Literally. He forgot work, forgot his still-lingering grief, forgot everything.

And as they rode one ride after another, Lance remembered why he'd always loved the carnival when he was a randy teenager with nothing but sex on his mind. In the small cars, spun by centrifugal force, Tamara's body was plastered against his most of the evening. It was a delicious, faintly sinful thing to slip his arm around her and feel the soft weight of a breast against his rib cage as the Teacup smeared her against him. She screamed and clutched him, and jumped off one ride only to want to go on the next.

She looked absolutely dazzling tonight. Her dark hair gleamed and swung at her slim shoulders, and the fabric of her shirt clung nicely to her full round breasts and slim waist. The lines of strain had eased and she looked young and free and delectably sexy.

Stumbling off a third thrill ride in a row, she said, "I think we need to do something tame and let my stomach calm down."

Lance flung an arm around her shoulders. "I'm glad you said that, sugar, because I might have had to do an unmanly thing if we rode another one."

"You should have said something!"

"Oh, no. I can't let some girl be wilder than me."

"How about the Ferris wheel?" she said, pointing.

"We can do that."

As they reached the line, however, Tyler, Louise and the boys joined them. "The kids are worn-out," Louise said.

"Mommy," Cody said, "can I spent the night with Grandma? Me and Curtis?"

Worry clouded Tamara's eyes. Lance bit his lip to keep from urging her to do something she wasn't comfortable with, but he wanted her to say yes. "Oh, I don't know."

"I'd really like to have him," Louise said. "But if you like, I can take them with me and Lance can bring you around to pick him up when you're finished."

Tamara wavered. "Are you sure you don't mind?"

"Heavens, no!" She grinned at the children. "We're going to have a fire and a story."

"Please can I spend the whole night? I like fires!"

Tamara bit her lip. Lance wanted her to say yes, wanted to have the chance to put his hands on her, to maybe even make love, but the conflict was too deep. "I'll take you over there when we're done and you can see how he's doing," he said. "How about that?"

She gave him a grateful smile. "Okay." She bent over and kissed Cody's head. "Be good, now."

He flung his arms around her neck. "Thank you, Mommy!"

As they walked away, Lance took Tamara's hand. "Do you still want to ride the Ferris wheel? Or can we go someplace a little quieter?"

Fear flickered on her face, and Lance cursed himself for pushing. "Quieter? What do you mean?"

"Never mind," he said with a smile. "Let's ride."

They climbed into the car, and settled in, a new awkwardness between them. Lance didn't try to touch her as they moved around, stopping at intervals to allow other customers to be loaded in. At one point, the whole wheel made a low groaning. "What was that?" Tamara asked in alarm.

"Just the machinery burping," he said, but his mechanic's ear wasn't quite sure. It sounded like a missed gear. When they came back around, he'd get them off. In the meantime, he didn't plan to worry her.

"Look at that," he said, gesturing toward the lights of the town, spread out below them, and winking in isolated hollows between the trees. "I remember when you couldn't see anything but blackness up there on the mountain. It's like a fungus, spreading over the earth."

She smiled. "You're the construction magnate," she said.

The wheel gave a jerk and moved up one more notch, putting them a little past midway. Lance listened for, but did not hear, the odd grinding.

Tamara made a soft noise and gripped the bar in front of them as the car swung faintly. "It's really high," she said breathlessly. "I haven't been on a Ferris wheel in a long time."

"All those wild rides, and not a peep, and now the Ferris wheel scares you?" he teased.

"Those others are all enclosed, and they just go fast or upside down."

As slowly as possible, so the car wouldn't rock, he eased closer and put his arm around her. "You can hang on to me."

Her body flowed into his, hip to hip. "Thanks."

"Ah-ha—it's a ploy, isn't it? You want to ravish me," he joked.

The car jerked upward, and Tamara clutched his leg with a fierce grip. This time the grinding sounded again, and Lance frowned. Definitely a skipped gear.

"What *is* that? I don't think I want to stay on."

Privately, Lance agreed. "It's nothing. I'm the engine guy, right?"

"Yes." The word was tight and closed, and her grip on his leg had not eased at all.

"Let me guess," he said. "You're afraid of heights."

"Bingo." She laughed. The sound was whispery. "Isn't that ridiculous, for a woman raised in the mountains?"

"Not at all. I read somewhere that vertigo is connected to inner-ear imbalances."

The wheel jerked again, but only moved a half a foot. This time, Tamara moaned outright. "I'm really imbalanced then."

Lance pulled her closer, wrapping both arms around her. She buried her face in his shoulder, and he could feel a faint trembling in her body.

And he thanked the stars or God or whoever it was that had arranged this moment. High above the earth on a clear mountain night, with this woman pressed so close against him, he felt an odd sense of peace. Of disconnectedness to anything but her.

The wheel jerked again, harder, and with a quick, stomach-wrenching movement, they sailed upward, maybe two positions. Then another. The car swung slightly, almost at the top. The wheel ground noisily, and Lance could see a crowd gathering, far below. He frowned when he realized the operator was unloading riders, rather than loading them on.

"What's happening?" Tamara asked in a faint voice. Her face was pressed tightly into his shoulder.

"We just have to get to the bottom and we'll get off." The worst that could happen was that the wheel would freeze. It wasn't as if the cars would come loose or anything of that nature. He was comforted by the fact that they were on the way down.

Even if it was a long, long way yet.

A shout came from below, and the wheel made a long, extremely loud grating noise. It moved one inch, maybe two. And stopped.

By the cursing below, Lance knew they were in for

a wait. He doubted it was anything serious, but he also doubted Tamara would take that news in stride.

She lifted her head. "We're stuck, aren't we?"

"'Fraid so."

Her face was white. "I hope I don't have to be sick."

"You won't," he said, and gently pulled her back into his arms. He stroked her back, and her arms, and felt her trembling begin to ease. Her breast pushed into his side, infinitely plump and soft, and Lance fought an image of her naked and pressed against him this way. His unruly member leapt to attention at the thought, and he shifted slightly to accommodate it.

To distract himself—and her—he said, "So tell me about the last book you read."

"The last book?" she echoed nervously. "Uh... *Accounting Procedures.*"

"No, not for school. For fun." Under his arms, she was rigid as a rock. "Surely you've read something interesting recently."

She peeked over the edge. Her fingers dug almost painfully into his thigh.

"Don't look down, sweetheart," he said. "Look at me. Let's just talk. They'll get us out of here safe and sound."

With clear effort, she dragged her gaze upward, and focused on his face. "Why do I torture myself with high rides like this when I know heights make me sick?"

He grinned. "You're a daredevil at heart?"

A ghost of a smile touched her lips. "That must be it."

Up close like this, her beautiful eyes full of fear and

bravery in equal measures, with her thigh next to his, and her warm body nestled against his, she was more than any man with a lick of sense could resist. "So, what was the last book?"

A frown wrinkled her brow for a moment. "Let's see...it must have been Alice Hoffman. It was a wolf story—I've been on a magical realism kick."

He smiled. "That fits."

"Oh?" She narrowed her eyes. "How so?"

"You're a very practical woman, but I see that wish for things to be magical in you."

"Are you a fan of those kinds of books?"

"Me? Not really." He lifted a shoulder. "I don't have time to do a lot of reading, but I usually go for suspense or horror when I do."

"Stephen King kinds of things?"

"Sometimes. He has great characters, but Dean Koontz has better romance."

She gave him an impish grin. "You like a little romance with your gore?"

"Exactly."

The Ferris wheel groaned, suddenly and loudly. Tamara jumped, her eyes flying to the ground. Instantly, she closed her eyes and took a breath. "What was the last classic you read?"

Silently, Lance cheered her self-control. She was scared out of her mind, but she was handling it. "Must have been something in college. I don't do classics." He chuckled. "I know you're surprised."

She looked at him. "Actually you do surprise me quite a lot."

"Do I?" he asked huskily—and snagged a kiss. Just

a quick, light one—and like an hors d'oeuvre, it only made him hungrier. "Like that?"

"No. I'd expect you to steal kisses. I wouldn't expect you to read much of anything."

"Everybody reads."

She laughed. "Not hardly."

"Well, in my family they do. We don't read the same things, now. Tyler is the only serious reader— the only one who feeds on literature and all that rot, but we all have our little corners of obsession. I can't sleep if I don't read for a little while."

"Really?"

He didn't know if he should be offended or not. Did he seem that stupid? He decided to let it go—the world was full of stereotypes about construction workers, and it was something he'd learned to live with. "My mother read to us every night before we went to sleep. It got to be a habit for all of us."

"That's great." Her hand had at last eased a little on his thigh, and she felt brave enough she put both hands on the rail in front of them. "Where did you go to school?"

"Rice. My dad wanted me to do Harvard or one of those big eastern schools, but I chose to go to Texas instead."

"Rice?" she echoed, faintly disbelieving. "I wonder how I missed knowing that about you."

This time, he could tease her. "You just think us pretty boys are only good for one thing. You forget about our brains."

She didn't smile. It seemed, actually, to disturb her. "With an education like that, why did you stay in construction?"

"That's easy. I love it." He gestured toward the mountain. "It causes me some conflicts sometimes, but there's a thrill in building things that I haven't found in anything else. You build something right and it can stand for centuries. Do it wrong, and it's an eyesore for even longer."

"I never thought about it like that." She smiled. "That's beautiful."

And even if it was what she expected, Lance couldn't resist. "So are you," he said, and kissed her again. This time, she kissed him back, eagerly, and he moved slowly to pull her close to him, cradling her head in the crook of his elbow, putting his hand under her jacket. "I love kissing you," he said.

"I like it, too." She lifted a hand to his face. "It makes me feel alive." And this time, she drew him close to her and put her lips against his.

Lance gave himself up to the spell she always cast over him. Gave himself up to the wild moment, trapped high in the night sky with this sweet and prickly woman. He moved his hand on her waist, restlessly, feeling a thick arousal burning through his groin. Slowly, giving her plenty of time to stop him, he moved his hand higher, brushing the lower edge of her breast.

She only lifted a hand to his chest and tilted her head to give him deeper access to her mouth, and Lance lifted his hand and covered her breast, cloaked as it was in the soft cotton shirt.

And he didn't know why he was surprised, but the flesh filled his hand exactly. He made a low sound at the discovery, and rubbed lightly across the nipple that nudged his palm. Her breath caught and she pulled away from his kiss.

He didn't move his hand as her gaze and his met, and caught. Feeling unlike himself, he slowly stroked the rigid point through her shirt, watching the reaction in her eyes. Her pupils dilated, and her lips parted on a gasp as he plucked it a little.

Her hand moved on his thigh, moved upward, barely teasing his erection through his jeans, and Lance kissed her again, unable to let her look into his eyes for fear of what he would reveal. With a soft groan, he moved his hand under her shirt, feeling electrified at the satiny texture of her skin. He explored a little, and moved back up, knowing she was shielded from view by her jacket and the great distance to the ground. He encountered her bra, and hastily tugged it out of his way, letting her breast fall from its case. The nubby flesh touched his thumb, and Lance grasped it.

And now her hand moved higher, moved to stroke him, as he ached to have her do. She, too, was stealthy and mindful of the crowd far below, so her movements were slow, firm—excruciating.

Just then, the Ferris wheel moved. It didn't grind or jerk, but simply started a smooth, slow descent. Lance jerked his hand away, as Tamara did. They lifted their heads.

And laughed. "Typical," Lance said.

Tamara grinned. The grin was edged with a hazy eroticism and genuine humor. "Curses." She shifted away from him as the car came to a stop at the bottom.

"Sorry about that, folks," the operator said.

Tamara stepped out and her knees nearly buckled. Lance grabbed her hand. "Come on," he said.

She made no argument.

Chapter Ten

As they walked away from the carnival, Tamara was aware of her heart racing a little in anticipation. Lance took her hand in his, and brushed against her, close, sending the aching sense of awareness up another notch. His hand was big and callused. He stroked her thumb restlessly.

They didn't talk. The only sound was gravel crunching underfoot, and the fading music of the carnival, and yet it didn't feel awkward to her. Her nerves hummed with the imagined pleasure of touching him, as much of him as she could—and letting him touch her in return.

He had parked his car between two semitrailers behind the grocery store. "Odd parking space," Tamara remarked. But it wasn't, not for their purposes.

"I don't like to leave her out anywhere. The trucks

hide her.'' He let go of her hand to unlock the door, and a thread of reason wound through her sensually hazed brain. Was she really going to neck with a man in a parked car?

The heat between them was vivid as a bonfire— Tamara knew they wouldn't get out of the parking lot, not with each of them in such an aroused state.

She hesitated, her hand on the door. ''Lance—''

He kissed her. His hand clasped her head, holding her close for the heady, fierce onslaught of his mouth. It left her dizzy when he raised his head, his eyes burning dark. ''Ladies first,'' he said. The raw need in his voice was the last straw.

Without a second thought, Tamara slid in, aware of a heady, almost drunken dizziness, and a roaring in her ears.

Lance climbed in beside her and locked the door with a strange deliberation of movement. Then he slid from behind the steering wheel with purpose, making a low, warm sound of anticipation, and kissed her— full mouth, full heat, full desire.

His passion sent her heart pounding into overdrive, and she clutched his shoulders, gasping for breath, her nerves clamoring for the feel of him, for his hands, his mouth, his body against hers. All night she'd been feeling aroused as he held her, as their bodies brushed and crushed and rocked together. All night she'd been wanting to kiss him, to feel his hands on her, to feel his body with her own hands.

And now she had the chance. As he thrust his tongue hungrily into her mouth, as she met those furious, deep kisses with a fierceness of her own, she found the buttons of his shirt and quickly released them so she could put her hands on his skin. On his broad, strong chest.

Supple flesh, lightly dusted with almost silky hair, met her questing fingers. She explored the planes of collarbone and the curve of ribs and the powerful netting of muscles over his flat stomach. Feeling stymied when her fingers tangled in the shirt, she made a sound of frustration and tugged the fabric from the waistband of his jeans, then plunged her hands under his shirt again.

A deep noise rumbled from his throat at her actions. His hand on her thigh gripped tight and his tongue plunged deeper, his other hand cupping her skull. He kissed her as if he were drowning, and her mouth the lifeboat, with a kind of desperate and mindless need that sent thrilling jolts of excitement through her body.

He felt so good, so right—the muscles of his waist, the sleekness of his flesh, the soft hair on his chest, the pinpricks of his nipples against her palms. She moved slightly, to kiss his chin, and his neck, and his chest. It smelled deeply of night and sin and promise—a man's smell. Never in her life had she felt this kind of mindless, pure hunger for a man. Never.

He gripped her head in his hands. "You're making me crazy, Tamara," he said in a growling voice. "Crazy," he repeated. "I want to feel you."

Tamara let go of him. "I want you to," she said, amazed and aroused by her own boldness. She began to struggle out of her jacket, and while her arms were trapped in the sleeves, he covered her breasts with his hands.

She went still, electrified by the sensation. As he stroked her breasts, dizziness swirled through her mind, and a pulse beat in her lips and breasts and between her thighs, at once urgent and slow. He bent his head with a growl and put his mouth over one nipple, soaking the cloth of her shirt and her bra with enough heat that she gasped. With his teeth, he gently seized the aroused point and nibbled lightly. Tamara cried out, and without letting go, Lance shoved the jacket from her arms, nibbling and nudging until she thought she would scream in pleasure.

The jacket went flying into the back seat. Lance pushed her against the far door. It was dark but for a single ray of light cutting a path over the top of one of the trucks, and very quiet.

His hands, both hands, covered her breasts, as he lifted his head and kissed her. Lightly this time, with that devastating, exquisite talent. His hands, too, moved with expertise. He slid his palms over her flesh, spreading his fingers to caress and weigh and gauge. He stroked her nipples as Tamara had stroked his, with his open palm, and Tamara moaned softly against his lips, plunging her hands under his shirt to feel his skin, to touch his back and his hair and his beautiful face.

He spread kisses over her face, pressing to her eye, her forehead, her chin, her cheeks, her lips again. And his thumbs and fingers splayed over her aching breasts, teasing and kneading ever so gently.

And then he made a deep groan, and reached for the hem of her shirt. Tamara didn't think, she only moved forward, away from the door, and let him pull it off of her, lifting her arms so he could tug it from her body. Carelessly he tossed it over his shoulder, his face sober with intent.

He lifted his head, and Tamara felt her breath go

still and deep and very far away as he looked at her in the dimness. With the tips of his outstretched fingers, he skimmed the flesh over her bra, tracing the curves from her shoulders to the edge of the utilitarian undergarment she wore, then pressed a trail of nibbling kisses to the path his fingers had taken. A lock of his hair brushed her chin. He kissed her neck, her jaw, her mouth, and lifted his head to look at her.

Pausing, as if to give her time to tell him to stop.

Tamara gazed back at him and touched his face, put her fingers on his mouth. "All I wanted, all night, was to touch you, and have you touch me," she whispered. "It's even nicer than I imagined."

He did not smile, but only shifted his gaze, and moved his hands to her shoulders. Very slowly he slid her bra straps down over her arms, stripping the fabric from her breasts an inch at a time, until she was unveiled to his gaze. She trembled as he unhooked the garment and flung it, too, carelessly over his shoulder.

It was not cold, but she shivered when his hands rose again, when his bare fingers touched her bare breasts, flickered over the tips. When he opened his palms and took the weight of her into his hands.

A quiet, mildly profane curse stained the air, and suddenly, Lance moved, capturing her by her waist, turning so he could settle her in his lap, her legs straddling the fierce, pulsing heat of his arousal.

"Tamara," he said, moving his hands over her back. His breath grazed her nipples and she shuddered violently against him, pressing the ache between her legs against the ache between his. "You're so beautiful and warm."

His voice, gravelly with need, slayed her. She kissed

his head, and touched his ears. And Lance, beautiful, skilled and wild, opened his mouth and suckled her breast.

She would die of the pleasure. It was fierce and bright and almost painfully erotic to be with him like this, his thick hair under her fingers, his beautiful mouth skillfully nibbling and nudging and suckling, as if it were the finest thing he could imagine to taste, as if he could do it all night, as if there was nothing, nothing he would rather do than lavish that minute, perfect attention upon her breasts. Upon every inch of the longing flesh, the aching tips.

All night. She rocked restlessly against him and heard him make a deep, yearning sound. Against her, he moved his hips. She clutched his shoulders fiercely, wanting it to never end, to never cease.

A wild pulse pounded through her veins, rocketing from her breasts to her groin, jolting higher and higher with every touch of his mouth or hands, and the lost, rough, pleased, sounds he made. Her body trembled deeply and she found her hands moving restlessly over him, into his hair, over his shoulders, on his arms. He moved beneath her, his hips creating a relentless, rocking pressure.

With a shock, she realized she was very near culmination. With a cry, she froze, but at that instant, he caught her flesh lightly between her teeth, and grasped her buttocks tightly in his hands. She made a soft whimpering noise, unable to stop the rising crescendo, not when he touched her like this, when he rocked against her like that, not when—

"Let it go," he said in a raw voice. "Please, let go, Tamara. Let me feel you come apart."

With a sob of release and mind-shattering pleasure, she did. She let him thrust against her, his fingers tight on her buttocks, his mouth slowing as if he knew. And when the spasm slowed, he pulled her close and held her, kissing her shoulder, stroking her back, his own need still raging and fierce against her slowing body. "I'm sorry," she whispered into his neck. "I didn't—"

He grabbed her head and kissed her into silence, his mouth as sweet and deep as a stream. "Never apologize, ever. It pleases me to please you."

"But—"

The sudden sound of glass breaking crashed into the still night. Tamara and Lance froze. A flurry of shouts could be heard.

"Damn," Lance said, moving quickly. "Get down."

Flung aside, Tamara crouched on the floor of the car, hearing the brutal sound of a fight spilling very close. Lance urgently started the car and backed out just as a bottle crashed into the side window. "Sorry, Tamara," he said, "hang on."

For a moment, she was too stunned, too awash in the lingering haze of sensual pleasure, to even think. She simply stayed down, crossing her arms over her naked breasts. Lights flashed over the ceiling of the car, over Lance, his hair disheveled, his shirt open down the front. She was riveted by the sight of him, driving wildly, a frown on his face.

The car came to a stop. Lance glanced down at her, and a wicked grin broke on his face. "Traffic light," he explained and grabbed her hand. Devilment sparked in his eyes as he leaned the slightest bit to brush his fingers over her breast. "This is a high-water mark for me, erotically speaking," he said with a slow grin. "How about you?"

Tamara ducked her head as the reality of the situation crashed in on her. "I'm mortified!"

He fell sideways. "Kiss me and you'll forget about it." Without waiting for her, he kissed her, his tongue sliding inside wickedly.

A horn honked, and Lance popped up again, chuckling softly. "It's only for another minute or two, sugar. Hold on."

The laugh tipped her off. She raised her head. "You're enjoying this!"

"Hell, yes!" He glanced at her, eyes glittering. "A gorgeous, passionate, half-naked woman in my car? What do you think?"

She crossed her arms. "I think men are sick."

Again his rich laugher filled the car, a heady sound that made Tamara wish she could enjoy it as much as he did, that she could overcome her sense of shame long enough to let down her guard.

"Here," he said, and braced himself to shuck his shirt. "I'll be half-naked. You be covered."

Gratefully, Tamara grabbed the shirt and put it on. "It isn't the same," she said.

But it was. There he was, naked to the waist, all that supple golden skin gleaming in the streetlights, his chest glittering with palest gold hair. He shoved a hand through his unruly hair, and impossibly, Tamara's stomach flipped again.

When he pulled out of the intersection, Tamara jumped up into the seat, trying covertly to fasten the buttons with her unsteady hands. The scent of his skin wafted out of the cloth, and the fabric felt like his hands on her. And she discovered, to her chagrin, that she had torn one of the buttons in her haste to touch him. The shirt gaped open in the middle, and Tamara tugged it closed, furious embarrassment flooding her like molten lead, burning away every second of pleasure she had known with him.

The litany of her sins spilled through her with painful humiliation: necking in a car like a teenager, riding through town half-naked, tearing his shirt like some wild woman—and worst of all, coming apart like that when he touched her, like some wanton sex fiend.

Faintly, she was aware of him next to her, aware of his body and his scent and the unfulfilled need that still hung between them. But she couldn't look at him—she was too desperately embarrassed.

The car came to a stop, and Tamara realized he'd pulled over next to the park, deep in the shadows. "You can put your clothes on here," he said, his hands on the steering wheel.

His expression was closed as he reached over the seat, scrambling in the back seat for her turtleneck, which he handed to her without a word, then her bra. He settled back in front of the steering wheel, face forward. "Go ahead and get dressed. I won't look."

Bewildered, Tamara frowned at him. Had she hurt his feelings? She clutched her clothes to her, hesitating.

Into her memory came a vision of herself, after Eric had rebuffed her attempts at foreplay. "Damn," he'd said, pushing her away. "All you ever want to do is go to bed."

Once, she'd taken great joy in the absurdities and

laughter inherent in making love. It always seemed to her that the act was worthless without a sense of fun, a sense of zest—though she supposed there were times it could be solemn. When you got right down to it, sex could be awfully silly.

Tentatively she reached out and touched Lance's arm. He bowed his head, but said nothing. Something about the nape of his neck, displayed by the scatters of hair that fell forward, seemed vulnerable.

"I'm sorry," she said quietly, moving close to put her cheek against his shoulder. His skin felt extraordinarily hot and smooth. "I got embarrassed. You made me feel so good, I went crazy, and when the mood got broken, I felt humiliated."

He lifted his head. In the low light, his eyes were somber. He took her hand and put it flat against his chest, holding it there by putting his own hand flat over hers. "You feel how my heart is beating?" he said. The gravelly sound was back—that rough, low, ragged sound.

She swallowed. "Yes."

"You're the sexiest woman I've ever met," he said. "I'd let you feel what else you do to me, but we don't have time now."

Tamara felt a wickedness of her own come to the fore, felt that lost sense of play returning. "You really won't let me feel?" With a smile, she moved her hand lower on his belly. "Even if I ask very, very nicely?"

His jeweled eyes flamed, and he pushed her hand down, lower. Tamara clasped him. "Very impressive."

"Don't tell me—" he said in a raw voice "—this is your revenge, right?"

She laughed—and the sound caught in her throat when he moved suddenly, trapping her against the seat by her wrists. "Two can play at this, you know," he said.

He kissed her, long and warm, and lifted his head. A perplexed expression kindled in his eyes. "I really like you, Tamara. I'm not exactly sure I think that's good."

Her breath caught. All at once, she realized she liked him, too. Liked his gentleness and his vulnerability and his street-scorching sex appeal, but most of all his ability to enjoy himself. "Why?"

"I don't know." He raised his eyebrows, and eased away. "I really don't know." With a sigh, he let her go. "Much as I hate to do it, we really should go check on Cody, see if he's going to spend the night or go home with you."

"You're right." She started to unbutton his shirt, to give it back to him, but Lance stopped her.

"Wait a minute." He swallowed and his fingers on her wrists drifted a tiny bit to touch her breasts below the shirt. "If you take that off, we won't be going anywhere."

"But I can't wear it in to your mom's house."

"No." He eased away. "I'll wait outside the car for a minute. Call me when you're dressed."

He needed the air, the air that had now gone chill with the mountain night, the air that filled his lungs and made him shiver without his shirt. He needed it to calm his racing heart, his raging libido, his soaring emotions.

What a woman! As the cold air did its work,

blowing away the strange, liquid hunger that had made mush of his thinking, Lance knew a sense of wonder. His instincts had not been wrong. Below that demure, slightly defensive and hostile exterior lurked a woman of singular passion.

He liked that she'd been able to laugh about their misadventure. Her embarrassment had been fleeting and somewhat understandable—and he'd been relieved to find out it was because she'd been so responsive to him.

He groaned, remembering. The taste of her, the way she threw her head back and clutched his hair, the furious, almost helpless explosion of her body.

With effort, he shoved the vision away. They would have another night, another time. Next time, he'd take her slowly; he'd touch every inch of her bare flesh, taste every millimeter of that quivering body until she was out of her mind. Then he'd take his own pleasure.

And start again.

Shivering, he called out, "Anytime, sweetheart! I'm freezing out here."

He couldn't remember ever feeling like this. It was a weird combination of things. There was plain, old-fashioned lust in the mix, but it went well beyond anything he'd ever felt. He didn't obsess about women like this. He didn't care that much, if the truth were told. He kept himself aloof. If he stayed aloof, he stayed out of trouble.

The truth was, for all that he was outgoing, he was essentially private himself. A woman like Tamara protected her inner self with a hostile attitude. Lance had learned to act as if there were nothing below his friendly surface.

And Tamara somehow reached below all that. When he was with her, he was aroused, but he also felt a strange kind of tenderness, a protectiveness. When he thought of being with her, he imagined holding her naked body close to his, but he also liked to think of holding her all night, next to him.

"Okay!" she called from within the car.

For a long, terrified moment, Lance didn't move—stunned by the clarification of his longing.

Ah, hell. He hoped he wasn't going to end up falling in love after all this time. Not with a woman like Tamara, who needed a solid, steady man at her side, some man to be a husband and a father, someone reliable.

Not a will-o'-the-wisp man like himself. He'd seen the damage his father's nature had wrought in the life of a woman who loved him. He'd vowed long ago not to ever do that to anyone. It was one thing to be a good-time Charlie, on your own. Quite another to drag a family down with you.

With a thickness in his chest, he got back into the car. Tamara was dressed again in the alluring blue turtleneck, her hair shining. He resisted the urge to kiss her again, afraid he really wouldn't stop this time. "Back to normal, huh?"

She lifted her eyebrows. "More or less."

The impishness in that expression nearly shattered his control again. With hands shaking from the effort of staying away from her, he started the car.

It would be hard, but he had to stay away from her. She needed to find a man who was real husband material. Someone like his brother Tyler, maybe.

His gut wrenched. No, not Tyler. Lance wouldn't be able to stand it.

Chapter Eleven

Louise sat in her rocking chair, watching the two boys sleep. It took her back to her days as a young mother, when all she'd ever had time to do was wash one face, fix another meal, break up a tussle, feed the animals and keep supper warm in the oven for her husband, who worked fourteen hours a day.

She missed those days sometimes. She'd felt important, valued, loved. Her boys needed her. Her husband, at least back then, had needed her, too—to keep him fed while he worked himself into a fortune, if nothing else.

A soft knock sounded at the back door. Putting aside the book in her lap, Louise went to answer it, expecting Lance.

It was Mr. Chacon. "I am sorry to bother you so late," he said. "But I cannot find how to turn on the heat."

"Come in," Louise said. Once again, she admired the thick black mustache, shiny and somehow sexy above the mouth that always seemed to be smiling. You couldn't tell exactly, but his eyes had a twinkle that certainly suggested smiles. "It's tricky, that furnace. You'll have to wait for my son to get back—he'll show you. Would you like some coffee, or maybe some hot chocolate?"

He lifted a hand. "Oh, no. I do not wish to be a problem to you."

"No problem. I'd be glad of the company."

"You're sure?"

Louise nodded firmly.

"Well, then, I would like very much a cup of chocolate."

"I like it with a little schnapps in it—how about you?"

He shook head with mock seriousness. "No, I will not drink liquor in the company of such a beautiful woman. My passion might overtake me."

She laughed, charmed by the twinkle in his eye as much as the outrageous compliment. "I'll try not to tempt you too much."

They sat at the broad pine table in the kitchen, and talked for more than an hour while they waited for Lance to return. Louise learned that Alonzo had come to the United States on a whim, hearing that there was work for adobe makers, and had gradually drifted farther and farther north.

"You have no family?" she asked.

"Three children, but they are all married now. My wife, she died of the—" he tapped his chest "—I don't know the English. She could not breathe."

"Emphysema?"

"Yeah." He tsked. "She worked in a factory. It made her sick."

"I'm sorry."

He inclined his head. "I missed her very much for a long time, but it has been five years. It is not so sad anymore. My children are happy. That's good."

In the long driveway, Louise finally heard Lance's car. He came in a moment later, wearing an expression she had not seen since his youth. It was sheepish, a sheepishness he tried to hide with a grin. With her alert mother's eyes, she took in the dishevelment of his hair and frowned.

But when Tamara came in, unable to hide her blush, Louise saw Lance take her arm protectively.

Louise smiled. "Did y'all have a good time?"

Lance's hand slid down Tamara's arm and closed around her hand, as if to give the woman strength. "We sure did. Rode the Ferris wheel and got stuck."

"Oh, no. Not at the top!"

Tamara widened her eyes. "Too close for me." Her smile, shy and beautiful, flashed.

"I'm afraid of heights."

Lance chuckled. "So is Tamara." He nudged her. "Or at least she pretended to be."

"He's so irresistible," Tamara replied dryly.

Louise gave her a wink. "He's always thought so."

"Hey, no fair ganging up on me." He looked at Alonzo. "Jump in anytime."

Alonzo nodded sagely. "I will."

"How is Cody?" Tamara asked.

"Sound asleep. I gave them a snack and a quick bath and they went out like a couple of puppies. I promised I'd make French toast and strawberries for breakfast.''

Tamara looked abashed. "He's never had a grand-mother. It's something I always wished for him."

"Well, since none of my sons show any signs of giving me any more, it's a pleasure for me and Curtis, too. The only reason we have children is to have grandchildren, you know."

"So I've heard."

Louise wanted to ask questions, wanted to probe a little, to see if there had been some past connection between Lance and Tamara. Heaven knew, he sure seemed to like her.

But Louise thought she'd know if Lance was hiding something. He was a terrible liar. If Cody was his son, he didn't know it, and that might doom the budding romance between Lance and Tamara. Whatever you said about her devil-may-care middle child, he'd always had a strong sense of fair play.

Tomorrow, she'd see if she couldn't get a little more information. For tonight—

Then she remembered. "Lance, you need to run down to the guest house and show Mr. Chacon how to light that old furnace before you run Tamara home."

"Sure. If it's okay with you?" he looked at Tamara.

Tamara went a shade or two paler as she cut an apprehensive look toward Louise. "I'll just go peek in on Cody."

She was hiding something. Louise would stake her life on it. She stood. "I'll show you where he is."

Tamara walked alongside Louise, down a luxurious hallway, thickly carpeted and hung with family photos. Everything was neat and prim, and Tamara thought with despair of her own haphazard housekeeping. She was too busy to keep things this neat.

"You have a beautiful home," she said politely.

"Thank you. I wouldn't have picked it for myself, but I have an army of help, so it's not too bad. One thing my husband was good at was making money, I'll give him that."

A lamp shaped like a bear glowed dimly in the bedroom, illuminating the two sleeping boys, side by side on a double bed. In sleep, the resemblance between them was not so marked, and Tamara realized once again that it was as much a matter of expression and carriage as physical similarities.

"I just want to give him a kiss good-night," she whispered.

Louise nodded. Tamara moved quietly over the floor, sidestepping stuffed animals and balls and a plethora of toy cars. Bending over, she pressed a light kiss to Cody's head.

He stirred awake instantly. "I don't want to go home!" he protested. "We're having strawberries for breakfast."

"Shh, you'll wake Curtis." She stroked his hair. "You don't have to go home. I just came to give you a kiss good-night."

"Okay. Grandma heard my prayers."

"Good." She gave him another soft kiss. "See you in the morning, slugger.

"Night." He was already back to sleep before she left the room.

"He's the sweetest child," Louise said. "We had a great time."

"Thank you." She felt better about leaving him now that she'd seen how happy he was. She knew Louise Forrest's generous, loving reputation, and she'd known Tyler for a long time, but it was still strange to let her boy out of her sight—even if it was into the hands of his own blood grandmother. "I'm glad it worked out."

"You know he's starting to read, don't you?"

Tamara smiled proudly. "Yes. He's very bright."

"My Lance read early like that. It was one of the reasons he got in trouble so much when he was in school. They couldn't keep the child busy enough."

A fist struck Tamara's stomach. Louise was fishing. If she hadn't figured it all out, she wasn't far from the truth. As calmly as possible, she replied, "I'll have to remember that."

"Where's his daddy? You divorced?"

Tamara chose her words very carefully. She did not want to lie to this woman. "He hasn't been around for a long time."

"I see. That can't be easy. Cody told us you go to school and I know you work at the Wild Moose."

"Yes. But I don't mind, really."

"We don't, do we, not for the children." Louise paused to look at Tamara. "I dropped out of college when Jake came along. I can't say I never regretted it, but I did finally get my degree, just four years ago."

"That's wonderful!"

Louise shrugged. "It was for me. It was the end of my marriage, but I think I made the right choice." She frowned, pursing her lips. "Seems to me I remember you—Flynn. Was it your mother who ran the cleaning service?"

"Yes." Tamara let out a breath at the abrupt change of subject.

"Well, of course. She did my house for quite some time. Used to brag about you all the time. You got scholarships left and right—weren't you studying at CU?"

Tamara looked down. "I didn't finish."

Louise said nothing. Her blue eyes, so much like her son's, seemed to penetrate deeply into Tamara's heart, to see the truth behind the simple words. Tamara felt ashamed for the resentment she still sometimes nursed over the loss of that dream, and felt it was written all over her face. She never, ever regretted Cody, but it was hard not to mind having to pay with her own life for someone else's mistakes.

And yet, now, she would fight to the death to keep her son. She would wait tables the rest of her life to see him grow up strong and happy.

"Things have a way of working out for the best if you don't give up," Louise said at last.

Life had taught Tamara that was not true in the slightest sense, but she wanted to believe it was true for Cody, that finally the cycle of poverty and single-parent families would be broken. "I hope so," she said fervently. "I want a better life for him."

"Don't forget about yourself in the bargain," Louise said, and led the way back to the kitchen.

Suddenly, Louise paused and turned suddenly. "I know what I was trying to remember," she said.

Tamara waited, a fist of apprehension in her stomach as she noticed the tightness of Louise's mouth.

"Valerie was kin to you, wasn't she?"

"Yes. She was my cousin."

Louise nodded thoughtfully. "It was sad, what happened to her."

"It was." Tamara hoped Louise couldn't hear her heart. It sounded like rifleshot to her, or drums. Loud, anyway. If Louise put that much together, how much longer until she remembered Valerie had had a baby just before she died?

And how long before she put Lance home that Christmas?

"Poor girl," Louise said, pushing open the door. "I always felt sorry for her. She was crazy about Lance, that's for sure. I was glad to see in the papers when she got married. It must have broken her husband's heart when she died."

Tamara let go of a breath and made a vague sound of agreement. She sometimes forgot that Valerie had been *married* just before that wild affair with Lance. Everyone assumed the baby she carried belonged to her husband—and he'd left town, so he wasn't there to defend himself.

To Tamara's relief, Lance was waiting in the kitchen.

"You ready?" he said, standing up with keys dangling in his hand.

Was she ever!

He dropped her off at her house. They had been quiet on the way down the hill. Lance walked her to the door, and Tamara knew she wasn't ready for him to come in. Not with so many disturbing things to think about.

He seemed to sense that. "I had a nice time with you tonight, Tamara," he said, smoothing her hair over her shoulders. "I'd like to take you dinner or something, if you'll let me."

God help her, but she couldn't say no. Not with him looking like Thor in the moonlight, not with that promise of heady pleasure in his eyes. "Okay," she said.

"I've got to go to Denver this week, but I'll call you next Sunday evening, and we can work something out."

That slow, deep quiver stirred to life in her body as he bent down to kiss her. She'd never kissed anyone whose mouth seemed to fit hers so perfectly. Or been kissed with such a heady combination of slow passion and heartbreaking tenderness. He lifted his head, his hand on her face, and for a moment longer, he looked at her. "Good night, Tamara."

"Good night."

She tried to go straight to bed. It was late, and had been a very full evening, after all. After a half hour of fitful tossing, she gave up and went to the kitchen to make a cup of tea. Carrying it into the living room, she put Bach on the CD player, and curled up in her chair.

To think.

Valerie haunted her. Every variation of every emotion she'd ever had about her cousin rushed to the surface tonight, muddy and indistinct. Love, sorrow, regret, resentment—all were there, all in a tangle of hues.

But foremost among them was guilt. And shame. Oh, yes, there was shame, a heaping scoop of it.

Tonight, when Louise had spoken of Valerie, Tamara had remembered why she had wanted Lance Forrest to come home all these years—for revenge. She had remembered how Valerie suffered in her unrequited love, and how bitter she'd become at the end.

How despairing Valerie had been at the last! Night after night, Tamara had tried to comfort her, tried to make her see reason. But Valerie wouldn't—or couldn't. She railed at the unfairness of a man running off and leaving a woman alone to raise their baby—even though she'd never tried to let Lance know she was having his child.

She had complained bitterly of the fate of beautiful women who were used and cast aside. Tamara had had a little trouble with that one—Valerie's vanity had been a source of friction between them for a long time, and it never let up. Valerie had always thought she was the most beautiful, the most desirable, the most passionate woman on the planet.

With a start, Tamara sat up straight, her tea sloshing over her hand. In the background, a minuet danced, making a mockery of her dark thoughts.

Was it possible Tamara found Lance so compelling precisely because he'd once been Valerie's boyfriend? That somehow, after all these years, Tamara was taking a revenge of her own on the cousin who'd caused her so many problems?

Maybe she hadn't wanted to get vengeance *for* Valerie at all, but *upon* Valerie.

A cold sweat broke on her skin at the thought. Surely she couldn't be that shallow?

She rubbed her chest, feeling there the knot of thick

guilt pressing into her lungs, taking away her breath, stealing all her joy.

Valerie had been selfish and vain and a gold digger. Tamara was old enough and wise enough that she couldn't deny any of that. But she had also loved Lance Forrest with something akin to obsession.

Tonight, Tamara had held in her arms the man Valerie had adored. She had kissed him and touched him and let him cast his spell over her senses with a kind of hedonistic hunger she had never known.

It had been sheer heaven.

It had also been wrong.

The truth was, Tamara had not given a single moment of thought to Valerie when Lance had so deliciously ravaged her senses. She had thought only of him, of Lance himself, with his jeweled eyes and gorgeous mouth and buoyant attitude. She had been thinking of herself, and the pleasure he gave so willingly.

She closed her eyes. The whole mess was entirely too complicated, riddled with little sins that piled up and piled up until there seemed to be no possible answer.

Lance had been wrong to allow himself to be drawn into an affair with Valerie a second time. But it had also been wrong for Valerie to blame her pregnancy on him, and then hide it.

It had been wrong for Tamara to entertain thoughts of revenge against a man who, by all Tamara could see, was simply a charming womanizer. He didn't lie or cheat or make bold promises he wouldn't keep to reach his ends. He didn't have to—he had to only be himself.

She sipped her cooling tea, frowning. Valerie always said that Lance seduced her with promises of marriage. Knowing him now, Tamara didn't see that he would have ever done that. It didn't jibe with the rest of him. Tamara hated to believe that Valerie had lied—but it wouldn't have been the first time. Her unstable cousin had lied quite boldly and without conscience if it suited her ends.

But that didn't change one simple, inescapable fact. Whatever she'd done, Valerie had loved Lance, and it was wrong for Tamara to take now what her cousin had most wanted. It was a betrayal.

It didn't matter that Tamara knew that if the situation were reversed, Valerie would have done whatever pleased her. Tamara's mother had taught her better than that, had taught her to adhere to her own moral code, no matter how others acted.

That moral code had insisted that Tamara come home when Valerie fell apart. It had insisted that she take her cousin's child and raise him. It now insisted she could not indulge her longing for Lance Forrest. Not even for the brief, shimmering time he offered.

Bleakly she carried her cup to the kitchen. She rinsed her cup and put it in the drainer, feeling the silence and loneliness of her house all around her. She wanted more than this. More than always being alone, always struggling, her only joy the few hours she could steal from the business of living to spend with Cody. She wanted the freedom to spend her days at work she loved, rather than work she only endured, and time to play once in a while, and freedom from the worry of wondering how she would make ends meet.

Staring out the window at a pool of white cast by

the streetlight, she pursed her lips. She was tired of doing everything alone. Tired of not having friends, tired of being afraid to dream of anything for fear it would be stolen like her dream of college.

With a sudden burst of insight, she realized she wanted a husband and more children and the warm, rich family life she'd seen in other families while she'd been growing up. She wanted Cody to have brothers and sisters, and dogs and cats, and suppertimes filled with love and arguments and laughter.

What was stopping her?

Why was she settling for an accounting degree when she hated numbers? If she was going to be a woman of modest means, why not shift her focus to something she would enjoy?

Why not apply to Denver again, and return to her degree? Why not become the teacher she wanted to be, instead of an accountant who was miserable going to work every day?

It made her almost breathless to think about it. And for the first time in almost five years, the mist of familial duty was swept away, to reveal the truth: Tamara herself had let herself be trapped into a life she didn't enjoy. While there had been reason to leave school, and she would not change that, her anger and resentment toward Valerie had been unbearable, and Tamara had shifted the blame inward.

Only she could change her life. Only she held the key to her own dreams, to the life she wanted.

It scared her. Shutting off lights as she went, she climbed into bed with a racing heart. Choices. She'd forgotten she had choices, and somehow the dilemma with Lance had reminded her.

She still could not choose him. One day, she wanted a husband and a father for her children, but she didn't want one like Lance. He was a charming man, pleasant to be with, and she hoped they could be friends once she confessed the truth about Cody.

But he wasn't marriage material. Nor would he ever be.

Soon, she would work up her courage to tell him the truth, and she would also tell him she could not continue with their playful relationship.

It was the right thing to do.

Chapter Twelve

She wouldn't see him.

Lance called Tamara Sunday night. All the way home from Denver, his head had been filled with snapshots of her. Some were memories—her dark hair reflecting the colors of the neon lights at the carnival, her shy smile, her unexpectedly earthy laughter...

And, well—her breasts. He couldn't help it. His mind returned over and over again to that moment high above the ground when he'd lifted his hand and found her breast had been made for him. He kept remembering the feel of her—supple and delectably sensitive to even the tiniest touch. He wanted to make love to her in the light, so he could see what he touched, and watch her face blur with passion as he cupped his hands around her luscious flesh once again.

He hadn't forgotten the odd sensation he'd had

when he got out of the car, that maybe he was in too deep, that maybe he had no right to be wanting this woman. Especially not with this kind of intensity. She deserved better.

But maybe she deserved a little fun, too. Maybe it wasn't so bad to just want to please a woman—especially one who seemed to come alive to his touch like she did. Especially when it seemed life had not been particularly kind to her.

Yeah, right. He heard the litany of justifications with cynicism.

He could justify himself all he wanted. The fact was, he wasn't going to leave her alone because he wanted her. It was that simple. It wasn't for her at all.

He spent half his time in a pleasurable haze, wondering what she was doing, what she was wearing, how it looked on her, the other half remembering how blisteringly passionate she had been. How richly she had responded. He had one vision of her, her head thrown back, her hair scattering over his fingers, as he moved his mouth on her throat.

It aroused him massively.

In fact, as much as he liked women, this kind of round-the-clock arousal was new for him. When he was younger, Valerie had whipped him into a frenzy at times—but there had always been a deliberation about the way she did it. He'd never been entirely sure she really enjoyed him. Even when she thrashed and hollered, he'd suspected a lot of it was sheer playacting.

It was hard to believe Tamara was even related. There was a guilelessness about Tamara he found refreshing, and there was no doubt in his mind that her response to him—that soft cry, that trembling, rocking, falling apart—had been utterly genuine.

His blood was fevered by the time he could call her Sunday night. And he was more crushed than he would have admitted to anyone when she declined his invitation. She sounded tired, and made apologies, but the fact was, she was too swamped with schoolwork to go out.

He thought he sensed a little reserve in her manner, but put if off to her preoccupation with school. He also reminded her to call Marissa.

Every night for the next week, he called. The story was the same all week long. She was too busy. She had too much homework. She couldn't spare the time. By Thursday, his persistence embarrassed him, and he called Marissa instead.

"Hey, good-lookin'," he said. "I have a favor to ask you."

"Only if I can ask one in return," she countered.

Lance felt the tension that had built in him ease a little. Marissa was a sunny, cheerful woman, and he loved the way she made him laugh. In spite of what Tamara had implied, Lance also knew Marissa was not the slightest bit attracted to him—she liked big, burly, hairy biker guys. Her father would approve far too much of Lance for him to be even remotely interesting. "Anything you want, doll."

"You first."

Lance drew an eye on a piece of paper in front of him. "Has Tamara called you by any chance?"

"She did. I helped her with her accounting." She chuckled. "I have to tell you, this woman does not have a head for figures."

Lance carefully added eyelashes to the almond-shaped eye. "So I guess she's really been swamped?"

"Are you going to get to the point anytime soon?"

"I want to go see her at the bar tomorrow night, but I don't want to be too obvious about it. I think—" he cleared his throat "—maybe I'm getting the brush-off."

Marissa laughed softly. "I get it. You want some female there to balm your bruised ego if she tells you to get lost."

Lance grinned. "Exactly."

"I can do that. But I can tell you, she wants you bad, big boy."

"Yeah, right. What's your favor?"

"I need someone to take me to a dance at the country club in a couple of weeks."

"The country club? I thought you scorned all that rich-girl stuff."

Marissa sighed. "The fact of the matter is, I'm sick to death of the sideways comments about diet and exercise from a certain blond bimbo in my acquaintance, and I want to shut her up." She made a frustrated little noise. "Mine's an ego favor, too."

"I'll make a spectacle of myself, adoring you."

Marissa giggled. "And you will, too."

"It'll be fun." He straightened. "Just let me know the date and time and I'll pick you up."

With the quick switch of weather so famous in the mountains, the season changed suddenly. On Thursday, Tamara had to leave her coat in the car when she got to work, and it was warm enough that she wished she'd remembered to wear something cooler than a heavy sweater.

By lunchtime on Friday, a cold wind had blown through, bringing with it a thick muffling of threatening clouds. By Friday night, it was snowing. Thick, white flakes that promised an early, lucrative beginning to the ski season.

It meant that work Friday night was slow. Very few of the locals would chance the roads on such a night, and those who did had designated drivers. A handful of ski-hopefuls drank margaritas in the early part of the evening, but even they grew worried when the snow didn't let up by nine, and left for their exclusive condos up the road.

Tamara took the chance to reorganize her area, cleaning out half-used bottles of sweet and sour, reordering cans of piña colada mix and kosher salt and new sponges. The few customers lived close and would walk home.

As she worked, humming along with the jukebox, Tamara congratulated herself for sticking to her resolve to stay away from Lance. It hadn't been easy. Every time she heard his voice—that sexy, cheerful, hungry voice—over the phone, she wanted to beg him to come over to her house right that instant. She wanted to agree to anything he asked if he'd only promise to kiss her again, touch her, let her touch him.

But she resisted. She pleaded an overwhelming load of homework. She heard his disappointment with a finger of mingled sorrow and relief, and stuck to her guns. She lasted all week without giving in.

Sooner or later, he'd get the message.

She told herself she needed to put some distance

between them before she revealed the truth about Cody. She needed to have some sense of control over herself and the wild attraction she felt toward him before she could take that chance and make herself so vulnerable again.

Someone dropped coins in the jukebox and Willie Nelson sang about a good woman who loved a man she didn't understand. Tamara smiled ironically.

As if on cue, the front door burst open, allowing a swirl of cold wind and suicidal snowflakes into the room. And as if he were a creature of the wind, Lance Forrest walked in with it.

Every single one of the careful rationalizations Tamara had built up over the long week disappeared— melted like snowflakes under the warmth of his presence.

He was beautiful. There was just no other word to describe the shining presence of such a man. His sun-fingered hair shone with a fresh washing, and fell around the collar of his worn jean jacket in defiance of any attempts at styling. As he came in with Marissa, he threw a casual arm around her shoulders and made a joke, and the pose made him seem even taller and leaner. The days outside on the job in the bright mountain sunlight had given his face a deep tan that made his eyes nearly glow.

And he moved like some creature of the forest, negligently at ease in his own skin, utterly sure of his place in the world.

To her despair, Tamara's hands trembled, and she had to wipe her palms against her jean-clad thighs. Why couldn't she ever remember how he really looked? If she could remember exactly, it would be easier to keep herself guarded, to review that perfection over and over in her head until it lost its power.

But it was impossible to remember it all. The way he moved, the way he smiled, that shining aura he carried, like a saint from a Renaissance painting. Distractedly, she wiped the bar with a towel and wondered if the models for those painted saints had been men and women with Lance's sex appeal.

They didn't take a table. Of course not. Instead, they walked to the bar. Lance tossed a leg over a stool and leaned on the bar. "Hi," he said. His bright blue eyes shone in unmistakable approval, and a strange, uncertain expression that pierced Tamara right through the heart.

"Hi," she said, putting cocktail napkins down on the bar in front of both of them. "What can I get for you?"

Marissa set her purse on the bar. "Just a Coke for me." She waved at someone across the room. "I'll be right back."

Both Tamara and Lance watched her head toward a table where a gigantic biker in black leather and chains sat by himself. He smiled happily when he saw Marissa coming, and jumped up to give her a bear hug.

Tamara chuckled. "Looks like you lost your date."

"She's not my date, exactly. She's here to make you jealous." He smiled. "Is it working?"

Tamara swallowed the truth, which was that it worked all too well. "If it's me who is supposed to be jealous, I'm afraid not."

The sudden flash of emotion in his face stung her a little. He lowered his eyes and plucked at the napkin. "Well, it was worth a try."

Trying to ease that wounded expression, Tamara said lightly, "It would be foolish to get too attached to a ladies' man like yourself, now, wouldn't it?"

"I guess so." He straightened. "Get me a beer, will you please?"

She gave him a bottle of beer and prepared Marissa's soft drink, then carried it to the table where she sat. On her way back, she was conscious of Lance watching her, his gaze washing over her body with an almost palpable touch that lingered with warmth on her mouth and breasts and thighs. She tried to ignore it, but there was no ignoring his hand when he reached out and snagged her around the wrist before she could go back behind the bar.

"Lance," she protested. "I'm working."

"There's no one here." He didn't let go, only spread his fingers over her knuckles. "You want to tell me what's going on?"

"What do you mean?" Tamara forced herself to look into his eyes. A mistake. She stood too close, and now she could read the puzzled little hurt, the passion, the yearning that burned in his irises. Irises that up close reminded her of a marble she'd once had, a blue one with floating streaks of amber. There was a whole universe contained in the bright, sharded color.

He lowered his lashes. The tips were bleached golden, and showed clearly against the slash of sunburned cheekbone. His lower lip looked a little burned, too. Vulnerable.

"You know what I mean," he said, holding her hand in both of his, his index finger restlessly moving over her nails. "If you want to give me the brush-off you could just do it and spare me making a fool of myself like this."

From this angle, Tamara could see the burnished crown of his head, and she ached to put her hand against the thick hair, ached to feel it on her fingers. She ached to kiss that sunburned lip. "You scare me to death," she heard herself say. "You're way out of my league."

"No, sweetheart," he said, and finally looked at her again. "You've got it backward. I'm the one way out of his league here."

And then, as if it were a movie, as if there weren't a dozen people around, he looped a hand around her neck and pulled her down to kiss her.

Caught off balance, Tamara nearly tumbled into him. She caught on his shoulders, trying to steady herself enough to pull away, to somehow extract herself—

But his lips were hot with sunburn, and he hadn't forgotten anything about kissing in two weeks' time, and she felt bewitched by the glorious taste of him. He claimed her possessively, hungrily, with such mastery that she forgot why it mattered that he was kissing her here, in a public place, while she was on duty.

There was only Lance, so big and so hungry, smelling of soap and a hint of after-shave and the evocative scent of the pine and sky and night that hung in his thick, clean hair. Against her palms, his shoulders were powerful and broad, and his strong thighs clasped the outside of her legs in an intimate embrace.

She didn't want to stop kissing him. His mouth was a wildly delicious place, and she wanted to explore all of it, wanted to stay forever clasped in the sinuous dance of their tongues. The more she tasted, the more she wanted to taste, the farther she slipped into the narcotic spell he cast over her senses. He smelled right. He tasted right. He felt right—

She shoved away, ducking her head to hide the shame that flooded through her. "Stop," she whispered, backing away. She covered her mouth, let her hair fall over her furiously hot face. "I can't believe—"

"Can't believe what, Tamara?" he said in a dangerously low voice. "That you want me the way I want you? Can you please tell me exactly what is so wrong about that?"

She yanked her hand away and whirled, taking refuge behind the bar. But once there, she couldn't remember what to do. It all looked so alien. She chanced a scan around the rest of the room, but nothing seemed to have changed. No one seemed to have noticed—or maybe they just didn't care—that the bartender was smooching with a customer.

"Tamara," Lance said. His voice was firm and low. "Stop running away and just face me with it, whatever it is."

For a moment she resisted. She tried to imagine there was some way out of this tangle of emotion. But there wasn't. Setting her teeth, she took a deep breath and moved to face him across the bar.

"You want the truth, Lance? This is the truth." She gestured to encompass the bar. "This is my life. I'm a bartender. You are one of the richest men in the county, maybe even the state. You're footloose and fancy-free, with no intention of ever settling down, and I'm a single mother with a child to raise." Once she got going, she couldn't stop. "I think you're one of the sexiest men I've ever seen, but that's not enough for me." She stopped, and rushed on. "I can't afford you."

He said nothing for a long space of time, only looked at her with an unreadable opaqueness on his face. Finally he pursed his lips, stood up and dug out a sheaf of bills. With strange control, he placed the bills on the bar, smoothing each one as he counted it. "I'll leave you alone, then," he said. "Have a nice life."

Tamara didn't know what she had expected. Maybe that he would argue with her, or give her one of those charming smiles and play some silly word game.

She didn't expect him to just stand up and walk away. And she felt a deep, almost tearing kind of regret at the strange, abruptly controlled movements he made. If he were any other man in the world, she would have said he was trying to cover up hurt feelings. She would have interpreted that faint flush as one of embarrassment. She might have—

"Lance," she said, helplessly, and stopped.

He looked at her, his beautiful mouth pulled to a tight smile. "Forget it, Tamara. It's not that important."

With a lump in her chest, she watched him thrust his arms into his coat as he walked, watched as he stopped to put a hand on Marissa's back and said something in her ear. Watched Marissa pat his hand and cast a covert look over her shoulder at Tamara.

Watched him open the door and stalk out into the snowy night without a backward glance.

Chapter Thirteen

Lance roamed his faceless apartment for hours, prowling the small, sterile living room with its rented furniture, to the kitchen with its single pot and plastic utensils, into the bedroom where not a single painting or photo broke the white walls. It was a sterile, lifeless place, and tonight it seemed to mock him.

What did Tamara know about rich? Rich didn't mean a damn thing. She was the rich one, with her warm, fragrant home, with its comfortable chairs and easy grace. With her son laughing, and the smell of dinner cooking and music playing.

And maybe that was the point. Maybe she sensed the sterility of his inner life and wanted no part of it. He stared at his bare walls and knew she'd never live anywhere for more than a week without putting her stamp on it somehow, without finding some way to make it comfortable and cozy and warm.

God, he ached for her. Her smell, her taste, her laughter. Her warmth. Even after the humiliating experience in the bar, he couldn't stop wanting her. The yearning was vague, unfocused. It centered around having her close to him, holding her small neat body against his chest, in his arms. He just wanted to touch her. Kiss her.

After four hours of pacing, he finally grabbed his coat and headed out into the night. Anything was better than pacing those same three rooms.

The night was beautiful. The first snow of the year drifted from a leaden sky, only faintly tinged with pink from the town's lights. He held up his face to the fat, twirling flakes and rejoiced in the fact that whatever else had gone wrong in his life, at least he was home again. Home where he belonged, where it snowed. He'd missed the hell out of winter in Houston. He'd been longing to come home for three years before his father's death, but as soon as the telegram came, he'd known, instantly, it was time. People had urged him to reconsider, to think about what he was doing, but Lance didn't go about life like that. He acted on instinct, and he'd rarely been proven wrong.

He ambled for a long time, walking the perimeter of the town. And it was no surprise to him to find himself on Tamara's walk, looking at her lighted living room window. She probably had not been home long—her car still ticked as it cooled, and there was only a light dusting of snow on the windshield.

He stood on the sidewalk in the dark, with his hands in his pockets, staring at the glow of lamplight against her drawn curtains. Outside, the snow fell in utter stillness save for the lonely sound of a train whistle crying out in the night.

Inside, he imagined she had brewed a cup of the lemony tea she'd given him once, and sat over her books. Maybe there were waltzes on the CD player. Cody would be asleep in his bed, tucked in and smelling of dampness from his bath. Or maybe she didn't have time to give him a bath on Friday nights. Maybe it was too late when she got home.

In the vague area of his chest was an ache he couldn't name. The visions of her warm house made him feel things he didn't know he'd ever felt—at least not since he was a child. His mother had made a warm, safe place for her children, as much as she'd been able to, anyway. His father had not always been the easiest man to please.

But then, his father hadn't been around much. He came home and raised hell, and went right back out again, and his mother smoothed things as well as she was able, making calm the stormy waters.

Part of him was appalled that he was standing out here in front of Tamara's house like a lovesick teenager. It wasn't his style. But then, not much about this whole thing had been his style, had it?

Snow dusted his hair, and his jacket, and still he did not move. Cold began to seep into his thighs through his jeans, and his ears and nose hurt. And he only stood there, staring at Tamara's neat, warm house.

Was he just grieving, was that what this weird loneliness was about? Was he realizing nothing lasted forever, that sooner or later it came down to the ties you made in your life? It was certainly one of the reasons he'd come back to Red Creek. He'd grown tired of being the alien, had wanted to come back to his own place, to the place where he knew things, knew the sky and the trees and the bugs and the smells.

Maybe his wish for Tamara was just another part of that. She was a hometown girl, the kind of girl a wild boy didn't notice, but got to wanting as he got older and realized he wasn't going to be young forever.

Abruptly, her porch light went off. It spurred Lance to action. He found himself moving up the walk, and almost rang the bell before he remembered Cody was sleeping, and knocked instead. There was an urgency in the sound of his hand against her screen door, and he stepped back, appalled. What was he doing?

Then she opened the door, and he knew. Her face was bare of makeup, and her hair was pulled back in a ponytail, and she wore only a flannel shirt and jeans and socks. Ordinary things. And just looking at her took his breath away. It took him long moments to gather enough air to speak. Tamara simply looked at him with wariness and hunger in her big green eyes, a wistfulness on her mouth.

At last he found his voice, though it was a roughened version. "Can I come in?"

Tamara stared at him with a mingling of terror and joy. His hair was damp with melted snow, and in his eyelashes, some of the thick flakes had stuck, giving his eyes a starry look. There was no smile on his mouth, no gleam in his eye. She might have been able to resist that.

Instead, he wore tonight the same expression that had torn away her defenses the night of his father's funeral. Lost. Lonely. Adrift. In desperate need of comfort and unable to ask it.

She pushed open the screen door and let him in.

He didn't even close the door—just flowed to her and gathered her close, so very close, and kissed her. His mouth was cold and his nose nudged her cheek with an icy touch and his down jacket still held the winter night, but it didn't matter. His kiss was hot, and his arms were enveloping and she sensed he would inhale her like oxygen if he could.

No one had ever wanted her in her whole life the way Lance wanted her right then. And she'd never wanted so much to give anyone like she wanted to give him herself.

Gently she moved away from him long enough to close the door. When she threw the dead bolt, he made a small, pained sound, and reached for her again. And again, she felt a sense of being wrapped, enfolded, truly embraced as he pulled her against his big, long body. He buried his face in her hair. "Oh, Tamara, I want you," he whispered. "So much. Don't send me away again. Let me love you."

She lifted her head and put her hands on his cold face, and pulled his head down to kiss him. "I won't," she promised. "I couldn't."

With a rough groan, he kissed her. And it was an almost violent kiss—bruising teeth and fierce thrusts and a drawing, hungriness that set her blood aflame. She tilted her head to meet him with the same unfettered passion, pushing his coat from his shoulders. He let her tug it off his arms and let it fall to the floor without breaking the kiss. He touched her body, his hands roaming her back and her buttocks and her thighs and her waist, up to her head and down again, as if he would touch her everywhere simultaneously if he could.

Tamara let everything go. Everything. For this one night, she was free of past or future, of hopes or wishes or dreams. There was only Lance, so beautiful and wounded and lost, needing her like she had never been needed, nor expected she ever would be again. Here was a man who asked nothing but her pleasure, who promised nothing but a full enjoyment of her passion.

And passion she had. Oh, yes. It rushed through her limbs and into her throat and mouth. It swelled in her breasts and between her legs. It made her hands tingle with the need to feel his supple skin.

She let her inhibitions fall away. Let herself feel him, all of him. His muscular back and the broad shoulders and his upper arms, so thick with his work. She kissed his clean-shaven, hard-cut chin and his neck that smelled of pine and snow and night, and the light furring of hair on his chest.

With a sudden, swift move, he picked her up. "I want you in a bed, where it's warm and comfortable. Tell me where."

Tamara pointed. "I can walk."

"Not tonight," he said, and carried her through the living room and down the hall to her room. It was dark. He put her on the bed, and Tamara felt a strange, pulsing anticipation as he reached for the small bedside lamp.

She had no time to protest. He tumbled her backward and straddled her thighs. The aggressive gesture thrilled her, and her breath caught high in her throat as she reached for him.

He caught her hands. "No, let me touch you." His hair fell forward around his face as he reached for the buttons on her shirt. Tamara, sensing his need, dug her fingers into the comforter, grabbing fistfuls so she could remain still.

He took his time. One button at time, with no hurry, until they were all open, and she felt a slice of air touch her stomach and chest. With a single gesture of both hands, he pushed the fabric away.

She watched him as he touched her stomach lightly, putting his palm against her belly. The expression on his face made her remember the night he'd kissed her outside the bar, as if he was truly seeing her, making himself slow down enough to be truly present in that very moment.

But it was not easy to simply lie there, her hands to her sides, as he knelt above her looking windblown and glorious with his tousled hair and broad shoulders and thick, powerful thighs holding her own immobile.

It was not easy to remain still when he reached for the front clasp of her bra and unhooked it, and then let the fabric lie there, as if he prepared himself for some greatly anticipated wish. She closed her eyes in a torrent of pleasure when he slid his hands under that scrap of fabric, brushing her aching nipples lightly, and pushed the bra away.

For long moments, only air and his gaze touched her, both swirling over flesh unused to such attention. She clutched huge handfuls of the comforter in her fists, and opened her eyes, afraid of what she would see.

"I wanted to see you like this, in the light," he said raggedly. "And touch you." To illustrate, he stroked each risen nipple with the tips of his index fingers. "I wanted to see your face when I did it," he said.

She met his gaze with effort, that blue, burning, hungry gaze. And all at once, she was fiercely glad to be with him like this, to see him shredded with desire for *her*. She reached for his thighs and curled her hands around them. "Lance," she whispered, "please—"

He bent over and kissed her, and his open shirt billowed out, letting his chest meet hers in an erotic brush of hair and masculine heat against soft female skin. He moved down her neck, to her breasts. "You're all I've thought about," he said. "For days. I can't sleep."

She clasped him to her, so overwhelmed with desire she wanted the clothes out of their way. "Please, Lance, I want to be naked with you. Take off these clothes."

He lifted himself up, still straddling her, and took off his shirt. Tamara touched his smooth, hard stomach. "You are the beautiful one," she whispered. And wickedly, she smiled and let her hands fall lower, to stroke his rigid member through his jeans. He made a low sound, and his eyes closed, and she drank in the way his face looked now, sensually hazed and extraordinarily beautiful.

He caught her hands and bent forward, pinning her completely, her hands on either side of her head, his legs firmly trapping hers, and kissed her. His chest rubbed her breasts, and she arched a little against him, needed more. He kissed her chin, and her throat, her collarbone and her chest.

And at last he opened his mouth on her breast, hot and wet and wild. The sensation was so fierce, Tamara cried out softly. She freed her arms and he cupped her breasts, lifting them to his tantalizing tongue and lips, to the swirl and suckle and gentle nip of his mouth. His blond hair fell around his face and touched her flesh, and Tamara thought she could gladly die, right then and there.

The urgency in her grew, and she could not bear to go so slowly. She reached for the button of his jeans. "Let's take off the rest of our clothes," she said.

"Oh, yeah." With a quick movement, he stood up and stripped off his jeans so fast, Tamara had barely shed her shirt and tangled bra before he was finished.

And then she couldn't move because she forgot what she was doing when he stood in front of her, splendidly nude. She could only stare.

"Oh, my," she whispered. He looked like a painting. Yellow lamplight caught on his exquisitely carved shoulders, and flowed down his torso, glinting against the golden hair scattered in an artful dusting on his chest. He was as golden as a god, made of sunlight and an exotic grace that seemed born of mountain winds. Even the sight of his arousal, full and slightly foolish and erotic all at once, only added to the almost painful impact of his beauty.

Her heart ached with it, and she felt she could not breathe, unless it was to breathe in Lance. The ache grew when she saw he stood there a little shyly, not proud and cocky as she might have expected. He waited, limbs loose, for her reaction, as if he were not sure she would be pleased.

She raised her eyes to his face, and let her wicked thoughts show on her face. "I don't suppose you'd consider just standing there so I could admire you awhile, would you?"

He smiled, his eyes lighting with that sweet brightness that was boyish and freeing and so alive. He dived toward her, tumbling her backward in his naked embrace, covering her with his long, warm body. "I bet we can think of something better to do than that."

Tamara wanted to burst then, burst with the feeling of him all around her, his hair against her cheek, his lips skating over her jaw and her neck, his hands restless, stroking her arms and her back and her stomach. She clasped him close to her, inhaling the scent of his warm skin, touching his hair and his strong back and the erotic round of his forearm, hot and threaded with a thick, pulsing vein.

"I need you, Tamara," he said in a rough voice, his fingers on the waistband of her jeans. "I want to see you, feel all of you."

"Oh, yes," she whispered.

Deftly, he stripped her of her jeans and panties. When she was as bare as he, Lance paused, moving his hand up her bare thigh, over her hipbone and waist. He lowered his sun-gilded head and kissed her breasts. "You're so beautiful," he said quietly, and lifted his head to look at her. There was a great solemnity in his gaze. "I wish I knew some poetry right now."

Tamara's heart caught. She opened her hand on his hard cheek. "You're poetry enough."

He kissed her, deeply, passionately, with that same

hungry need that had inflamed her earlier. He caught her body close to his, tangling his legs and hers, wrapping her in his arms. Any play that there had been between them fell away, leaving only raw need, pure and intimate and overwhelming. Tamara let herself flow toward him, let her heart and mind and soul become enmeshed in the fierceness of his need, of her need.

When he moved over her, sliding his legs between her thighs, there came a quiet between them. Bracing himself on his elbows, he kissed her very gently, and plucked a condom from the pillow where he'd put it. "Will you do the honors?"

"Yes." There was a fine trembling in his limbs. She took the condom from his hands. He sat up to allow her to adorn him, and for one devastating moment, Tamara was overcome with him—with the feeling of him so close, and the expanse of his heated chest so close to her face, and the vulnerable trembling she felt all through him. She swayed forward and kissed his ribs, right over his heart. "Come home, Lance," she whispered, and drew him down with her, opening herself to him.

And she realized then that she was shaking, too, as if she were afraid. She trembled with such violence and aching want, that for a moment, she wanted to weep with it. Then Lance was around her, over her, in her. He moved with exquisite control, sheathing himself to the hilt. And stopped.

He lifted his head and pressed an achingly gentle kiss against her lips. His blue irises were unstable, rolling with a thousand things Tamara could not read, and she had the sense that he wanted to speak, to say something, but instead he closed his eyes, supped again of her lips and began to move within her, his hands clasped with fierce gentleness around her head.

Tamara could not think, could not breathe. She only moved with him, marveling at the fit of him to her, as his lips had fit hers, as his hands had fit her breasts. It was the most perfect moment she could imagine, embracing him deeply. Her precious, gilded, lost Lance.

And as they moved, deeper and closer, yearning for wholeness, Tamara realized with an almost piercing sorrow that she loved him. As she tumbled into completion, feeling him come apart within her, she bit her lip to keep from crying out the words, and only clasped him tightly to her, his head against her neck.

Because she could not love him. She could not.

Lance did not go home. He stayed in Tamara's bed all night, holding her, loving her, until both of them fell into a sated sleep.

Near morning, something awakened him, and he jolted awake into the stillness of the dawn. Cold, snow-tinted light pushed at the curtains over her windows, but he was warm next to Tamara. She slept on her side, her back to him, nestled close, and he had his arms around her. It was incredibly satisfying to simply wake up here, cozy under a heavy quilt, with Tamara in his arms.

He closed his eyes with a sigh, pressing his forehead against the flesh between her shoulder blades. Her skin smelled faintly of their mingled scents, and it was soft against his brow. He simply reveled in the feeling, the sweet, deep sense of relief he felt, and hoped he could go back to sleep.

But he couldn't. He was too aware of her alluring nakedness, her soft skin just under his palms, the warm weight of a breast pushing against his forearm. He eased away, trying to resist the temptation to kiss her awake, and propped himself up on one elbow to watch her sleep.

Pale light caught on her dark hair and made pearlescent tracks over her flesh. He let his gaze wash over the curve of her neck and the vulnerable place just below her ear. The lines of her back, the long curve of her spine and the exquisite arch of her shoulder blades, seemed at once to be almost unbearably graceful, and it was those simple lines that proved his undoing. At first he only touched her spine with his finger, very lightly, and traced the shoulder blades.

But then he wanted to put his mouth against them, and he moved close to do it, just putting his mouth gently against each tiny rise, tracing her spine to the back of her neck. In sleep, she moved a little, nudging her bottom closer to him, bumping his arousal. Drawn by almost narcotic longing, he moved his mouth to her shoulder, then to the vulnerable place on her neck. She made a soft sigh and he ceased, waiting to see if she was awakening, but she was not. She only moved restlessly, and her foot moved against his shin.

But her movements had put one rosy-crowned breast within reach. He bent his head to that crown and tasted it slowly, closing his eyes so only his mouth and her nipple existed. She shifted, and her hand fell in his hair, pulling him closer. He loved the taste of her, and let her know it, not hurrying, just tasting and nudging and rolling her flesh in his mouth, loving the low sounds of pleasure she made.

She turned toward him, sleepily awake now. "Lance," she whispered. "Cody will be awake any minute. We have to stop."

He pressed his face to the soft, fragrant valley between her breasts. "Okay," he whispered, kissing her lightly. He moved his hand down her belly, down to the soft curls there, and slid his fingers between her legs, careful to be gentle. "One more time, to remember tonight," he said, and it was a much more ragged sound than he would have liked. One more time for her? Or for him?

He found her moist and ready, and he felt a jolt of almost dizzying need. She was the most responsive woman he'd ever known—deeply, genuinely passionate. And she didn't take it all too seriously. All night she laughed and teased with him.

As she did now. She moved closer, touching his chest. "Well, if you insist," she said. Her hand closed around him.

"I don't have any more condoms," he said, aching with the need to be in her one more time. Just one more time this morning—to see him through until tonight.

She gasped softly as he captured a nipple that strayed close to his mouth, too close and tempting to resist. He grazed it with his teeth and she arched against him, her hand closing alluringly around him, making him groan.

"We'll just have to make do, then, won't we?"

And they did.

And this time, laying sated in her arms, Lance finally realized he was in trouble. Big trouble. Tamara Flynn was intelligent and strong and sexy. She had a sense of humor and a bawdy spirit that he doubted would ever tire him.

She was exactly the kind of woman he always avoided. The kind of woman he didn't want to hurt with his wandering ways. The kind of woman who deserved a lot better than Lance could give.

And he'd taken her anyway, had given implicit promises he could never keep. A woman like this didn't sleep with a man for fun. She didn't just take a lover for the heck of it. Women like Tamara saved themselves for a good man, a man who would care for her and love her and her children for the rest of his life.

With a crushing sense of despair, he realized she was already a single mother. Some other man had done this to her in the past. Someone had loved her and left her, leaving her to bear the consequences of that passion alone.

Some other man. The thought of it gave him a sick feeling. He felt murderous and jealous and trapped all in the same moment.

What a dog he was! Like a greedy rake, Lance had been unable to resist seducing her. Instead of simply allowing himself to enjoy her goodness, accept her friendship, he'd had to take it all.

Guilt washed through him with a doomed clang.

"Lance?" she said next to him, smoothing a lock of hair from his forehead. There was bewilderment in the word.

Yeah, he thought miserably. *I'm a first-class bastard.*

Just like dear old Dad.

Playfully he patted her bottom, as if there was nothing wrong. As if he were the man she needed, rather than the worst thing that could possibly happen to her. "Cody will be up and around any minute. Better get dressed."

Chapter Fourteen

Tamara peeked in on Cody and saw that he still slept deeply in the snow-dimmed morning. She was relieved to have a little chance in which to collect herself before the day roared to a start.

She ran a very hot shower, letting the bathroom fill with steam. It was very cold, and she shivered in her thin bathrobe. As the room filled with steam, she let the full knowledge of the night that had just passed fill her. She let the rich memories glide through her, gild the edges of her mind.

And then, as she took off her robe and stepped into the hot spray, she let it go. As long as she lived, she would remember this night. It had been precious and she knew on some deep level that it had been right. As right as anything she'd ever done.

But now she needed to face reality.

First of all was that terrible moment when she had realized that she was way past being infatuated. She was in love with Lance Forrest, with his energy and cheer, with his sweetness and passion. Even, damn him, with his freedom.

She didn't expect declarations of love this morning. She imagined he would be his usual cheery self when he emerged, and he would kiss her pleasantly, eat breakfast and be on his way. He might call her again— in fact, he probably would. He genuinely liked her. And last night, wounded and lonely, it had been to Tamara he'd come. She wasn't foolish enough to discount that.

But as she dressed, she knew she couldn't see him again. She couldn't bear to be in some middle place with Lance, never knowing when he would tire of her. She would grow shrewish and jealous, and all the fine beauty they had shared last night would tarnish.

Far better to accept last night as the rare jewel it was.

She looked at her face in the mirror and saw how solemn she looked. Because she loved him, there was one more thing she had to do.

Lance had to know the truth about Cody. It was way past time to tell him, to give him a chance to be a part of his son's life. She couldn't lie to him anymore. Before he left this morning, she would take him aside and tell him.

Buoyed by the decision, she went to the kitchen and started a pot of coffee, shivering in the cold room. On the way to the living room, she turned up the furnace, then pulled the drapes.

And gasped. It was still snowing, thick, fat flakes

that seemed in no hurry. They fell from a leaden sky, floating dreamily in the windless air.

But in spite of that airy look, everything was buried in the heavy, wet flakes—ground, street, houses. Her car was an unrecognizable lump. Trees drooped under the weight; the leaves that still clung to many branches held too much of the snow. Even as Tamara watched, a thick branch on the elm across the street gave way with a crack and joined several others on the ground nearby.

They called these storms tree breakers for a reason. Every couple of years, an early-winter or late-spring storm blew through the state before the leaves had had a chance to fall or, in the spring, after they'd leafed out. The leaves caught far too much of the wet snow, and entire branches snapped like twigs. The falling limbs would take down power lines, block streets, crush cars and break windows. It wasn't much of a problem in the mountain communities, but the cities along the front range would clean up the mess for weeks.

"Wow!" said an awed four-year-old voice behind her. "Is it Christmas?"

Tamara chuckled. "Nope. But maybe we can have snow ice cream this afternoon. What do you think?"

"Okay! And can I go sledding?"

"This might be too wet for sledding, but we can try." She kissed her son's blond head. "Let's go get you some breakfast, huh? How about waffles and sausage and hot chocolate to get you warmed up to play outside?"

"Cool," Cody said, doing a little gleeful dance in his footed flannel pajamas. There was something searingly like Lance in the quick exuberance, and a sharp pain pierced Tamara. She should have told Lance the minute he appeared. He shouldn't have to miss this boy's growing up. She could think of few things crueler.

She was putting the first batch of waffles on the table for Cody when Lance ambled out. "Smells good in here."

"Hi!" Cody said with delight. "Did you spend the night at our house?"

Lance grinned at the boy. "I sure did. It's a secret though. Can you keep a secret?"

Tamara took a breath against the acute pleasure of having him there, in her kitchen, on a snowy morning. He looked appealingly rumpled, and for one tiny heartbeat, she allowed herself to imagine how it would be if he were her husband, if she had washed that shirt and folded it to put in a drawer in a bedroom they shared. If he were her husband, he would be with her every morning before work, and she would cook for him, and every morning he would give her that bright, mischievous look he was giving her now, and bend over, and say, "Good morning," his mind clearly full of the night they had spent.

As he did now. She held the mixing bowl in her hands, against her stomach, and imagined his hand would always curl around her neck and he would always give her a husbandly peck before breakfast.

But the press of his lips was anything but a peck. He kissed her with more yearning that she would have expected to linger, with a heartbreaking sweetness. Slowly he lifted his head and she glimpsed in his eyes regret and longing in almost equal measures. "I always forget, between one minute and the next,'' he said, brushing his knuckles over her cheek, ''how very beautiful you are.''

Before she could speak, he was moving away, taking up a place at the table, snitching strawberries from Cody's plate. Tamara stared at the wide expanse of his back beneath green-checked flannel and knew she had to get him out of her life as soon as possible. She had to find a way to rebuild her walls.

Lance hated the way she looked at him all through breakfast. Warily, as if he were a dangerous animal who'd wandered in during the storm.

He hated the way she avoided his gaze, lowering her eyes quickly if he caught her looking at him. He hated the way she kept the food or the dishes or Cody between them like a veil. He could see through it, but couldn't reach her.

It made it impossible for him to know what she was thinking, what she was feeling. What she thought about last night.

Last night.

He didn't know what had happened. How he'd gone from pacing in his faceless apartment to taking refuge in Tamara's arms. He didn't know why his feet had led him here, why it had seemed to be the only choice.

All he knew this morning was that he'd never experienced anything like it. He hadn't know sex could feel like that, so rich and deep, so different.

He also knew he'd done Tamara a great wrong. He'd lain in her bed, smelling the scent of her hair in the pillow, his hand roaming over the sheet where she'd lain, and told himself he had to let it all go. She wasn't the kind of woman who could play his game. She'd told him that in the bar last night.

Lying there, unwilling to leave the warmth of her soft bed, he'd listened to her talking to Cody and clattering pans, and told himself he had to cut this as short and clean as he could. As gently as possible, he had to find a way to tell her it had been a mistake, him coming here last night.

Then he'd come to the kitchen to see her standing against the sink, and everything had flown out of his head. All his resolves, all his careful planning. She had been so beautiful he couldn't resist her, and her eyes had carried such warning and suspicion, he'd wanted her to know he didn't take her lightly.

With a growl of frustration, he bent his head to his fists, silently calling himself every name in the book.

Cody rushed through, bundled like a teddy bear. "Bye!" he said, clomping through, "I'm going outside to build a snowman."

Lance chuckled in spite of himself. "Build one for me, too."

"I will."

Tamara called out a warning to him. "Don't stay out too long." She closed the back door, and flipped the curtain aside to keep an eye on him. "Thank goodness for fenced yards."

She settled in the chair at the table and leaned over. "Lance, we need to talk," she said.

"No," he said. "Don't take it all apart." He touched her hands and let go. "Just let it be."

"Lance—"

"I don't want to spoil it, Tamara. Please."

A curious and fleeting vulnerability danced over her eyes and was gone. "Listen," she said.

He looked down, feeling a thickness in his chest. Hadn't he been going to tell her himself that he thought it was a mistake? Hadn't that been in his mind all morning? So what difference did it make if she did it?

"It's not about last night, Lance," she said. She cleared her throat. "It's about Valerie."

"Valerie?" He frowned. "What does she—"

She gripped his hands. "Please listen. It's important and I'm afraid to tell you, but you have to know."

He learned forward, alerted by her somber tone. By her worry. "What?"

Tamara looked out the window and back to him. "Cody is her son. I adopted him when she died."

Lance lifted his eyebrows, but he was still puzzled. Why did she have to tell him this now? Right now, this morning, with that worried frown on her brow? "I don't—"

And then suddenly, he thought he might. He remembered that Christmas when he'd come home. One cold December night, he'd run into Valerie at a bar, and one thing had led to another. She'd reminded him of a simpler time in his life. And although he'd told himself he shouldn't let himself fall under Valerie's spell, he'd gone ahead and done it anyway. When she was up, she was so wild and vibrant it was hard to resist her. It had been three weeks of up—then she'd crashed into one of her black moods. Rather than risk his health or his car to her rages this time, he'd headed back to Houston and never looked back.

A creeping cold filled his limbs, freezing his organs

and gut. He stared at Tamara, and everything about her seemed strangely acute: her green eyes, the fall of dark hair, her sober, serious mouth.

It never had really made sense that she didn't speak of Cody's father. There had been, from the beginning, something off kilter about the whole business.

"Why are you telling me this?" he asked. His voice was flat.

Tamara swallowed. "Lance, Cody is your son."

He closed his eyes. Even though he'd expected the words, the actual spoken sound of them was shattering. Before she said them aloud, his life was as it always had been. After they marked the air, everything was irrevocably changed. His whole life shifted.

Everything.

He couldn't look at her. "Why didn't you tell me before this?"

"I—" she began. The pause lasted so long, he finally had to look at her, hard, to make her tell him. She met his gaze without flinching. "I honestly don't know."

"So why did you pick this morning to tell me?"

Her lids fluttered down over her eyes, hiding her expression. "Because it wasn't fair not to tell you."

"But why now, Tamara?" Anger, pure and hot and unfocused, welled in him. "Why this morning, when you know it's going to change everything that happened last night? Why now?" He stood up so quickly, the chair tumbled backward. He caught it before it fell to the ground.

"I don't know!" she cried. "I honestly don't. I haven't ever thought clearly about any of it. I took

Cody because I loved him, and I thought you were so terrible for such a long time, but now—''

There was such misery in her voice that he felt his anger seep away as quickly as it had come. ''But now?''

She took a breath and blew it out, and met his gaze. ''Now I know you. And it isn't fair that you've been deprived all these years.''

No, it wasn't. But he didn't feel anything. Why was that? He couldn't feel anything except a howling sort of pain that had no roots or direction. Why did it hurt? And what hurt, exactly? That she hadn't trusted him? That she had saved it for this morning, then used it like a wedge to keep distance between them, when all he wanted was to get close again?

All of it.

''Damn her to hell and back,'' Lance said, finding a focus for his anger as Valerie came to mind. ''Why didn't she let me know? She knew where I worked in Houston. She knew my folks. Was she just going to hide it forever?''

Tamara shook her head sadly. ''On that level, you should be thankful. She got…well…pretty bad toward the end. Pregnancy seemed to make her worse. And after Cody was born, she just wasn't in her right mind ever again.''

''Meaning she blamed me, that she planned to extract revenge,'' he guessed. ''Am I right?''

''Yes,'' Tamara said quietly. ''She really hated you. And I…I guess I blamed you, too. For a long time.''

''Do you blame me now?''

She raised her face. ''No.''

Numbly he walked toward the back door and

watched Cody romp in the snow, a blue bundle of stuffing. *Your son.* Lance remembered the night when he'd thought of Tyler, and how much Cody resembled him. And the night at the carnival, when everyone had made such a big deal about how much Curtis and Cody looked alike.

No wonder.

But he didn't feel a big swell of fatherhood come over him. He didn't feel immediate, fulsome love for the boy. He'd been fond of Cody since he'd met him—he was bright and sweet and adorable.

He turned to Tamara. "I don't know what I'm supposed to feel right now."

Her smile was kind. "There aren't any rules, Lance. And I didn't tell you so you'd have make some big decision right now." She sounded stronger now, clearer. "It's very important to me that you don't feel obligated to do anything. I just wanted you to know."

He made an impatient noise. "How can you expect that I wouldn't feel obligated? Especially when I've hated how you had to struggle. It really doesn't seem fair that you've carried this load all this time, and he's not even your child."

"Oh, but he is my child," she said. "I was there the day he was born, and I haven't been away from him for a day since. I'm the only mother he's ever known." She swallowed. "Don't take him away from me."

And at last the fog cleared—or a little of it, anyway. Enough that it finally penetrated how frightened she was, how much it had cost her to tell him all this. He crossed the room in an instant and knelt before her.

He took her small, work-worn hands in his own and

kissed each one gently. A wave of emotion—something hot and jumbled and powerful—filled his throat, and he couldn't speak. He thought of her giving up all her dreams to come home to Red Creek and take care of his son. He thought of her poring over the hated accounting texts and working in the bar to make ends meet—because she loved Cody. "You're such a good mother, Tamara. I would never take him."

He bent his head and put his brow against her hands. "You sacrificed so much, I can't stand to think of it."

She freed one hand and put it on his head, in his hair. He sighed, feeling relief course through him. Maybe she wasn't using the whole thing to put a wedge between them, he thought. And then he was frightened because he wanted so much to come back tonight, and the next night, and the next.

He really tried not to want things. Anything. It was a lesson he'd learned at his father's knee. Olan had showed up when he felt like it. He didn't remember promises to take his child fishing, or out on a hike, or for a drive to see the aspens. Lance had learned after too many bitter disappointments to accept whatever came.

Lance had finally learned not to make plans, not to worry about the future—not expect anything. That way, he was never disappointed. When his father would appear with an open Saturday morning to take Lance fishing, Lance had been free to go with him, and enjoy it.

Sitting now in Tamara's kitchen, smelling the lingering scent of golden waffles, he didn't want to think about coming back. He didn't want his heart all caught up in her dreams and wishes. He didn't want to disappoint her. And he didn't want to want her—

He straightened. "I'll talk to my accountants and work something out, so you don't have to live like this."

"No, Lance, that's not necessary. I've done—"

"Don't be ridiculous, Tamara. I've got money enough for ten people, and I don't want Cody to have to go without. Or his mother." He raised a warning hand as she opened her mouth. "I know you've done the best you could, and I'm amazed you've built the kind of life you have on the shoestring I know you're living on."

She was blushing, deeply. "It's not that bad," she said, and he heard the humiliation in her voice. "I didn't tell you so you could throw money at us."

"I know that." He sighed in impatience. "One thing you need to get over is feeling like you have to scale the walls of the world all by yourself. It's okay to have a little help. It would make me happy to do that much anyway."

She nodded, reluctantly.

Silence fell and grew. Tamara broke it by taking his hand. "There's one more thing, Lance."

His gut clenched. Here it came.

"What we had last night was precious and rare." She paused. "But it can't happen again. I like you too much to let myself fall in love with you."

If she had said anything else, anything, he would have argued or cajoled, or even run away. But put like that, there was so much respect and honesty that he had no recourse. She was right to make this call—she saw him as he was, and he liked her for that.

Still, something in him ached. He reached out and touched her cheek. "You're right," he said. "I like you, too. Too much to do you wrong—and I would, eventually." A small bitterness twisted his mouth. "The apple doesn't fall far from the tree, after all."

He thought he glimpsed the faintest trace of tears shining against the brilliance of her irises, then it was gone. She simply nodded.

Lance stood. "It's been quite a morning," he said. "I think I need a long walk to sort through everything. I'll call you when I've talked to the accountant." He cleared his throat and looked out to the churned snow in the backyard, where a roly-poly figure rolled. "I'd like to start getting to know him as soon as I can. I hope you won't mind working something out so I can be a part of his life." He looked at her. "My own father wasn't there for me, and I always vowed I'd be there for my own children. Not—" he grinned ruefully "—that I really thought I'd have any."

She smiled. "That's fine. It will be wonderful for Cody. I think for your mother, too."

"Yeah."

As if sensing his need to flee, Tamara stood up and carefully pushed in her chair. "Well, I'm glad we can be civilized about it. If you like, I'll let you decide when you tell him."

Civilized?

For a moment, Lance could only look at her. At the sleek line of her hair and her lovely shoulders, and the sweet line of breasts. He was seized with a vision of her last night, lying like a sleek cat in the pool of yellow lamplight, her face awash with a rosy flush of passion.

His body responded with a furious, instantaneous reaction, and he found himself clenching his fists. She turned back and caught him staring. An answering flare lit her eyes for an instant, and was gone. She crossed her arms. "Lance, I mean it."

He licked his lips. "I know," he said. "Nobody said it was going to be easy." He moved closer, and trapped her with his body against the side of the refrigerator. He pressed close, feeling her soft breasts nudge his chest, her thighs so long and lean against his, her quick, excited breath against his neck. "Just one kiss goodbye."

"Lance," she whispered, dropping her head away from him. "It only makes it more difficult."

"Maybe." He brushed a lock of hair from her temple, and touched the thin skin there with his fingers, absorbed in the beauty of the place, amazed at the tiny blue shading of veins. "But maybe it will just be a very, very sweet goodbye."

He kissed her temple and heard her breath catch, even as she moved a little, almost unconsciously, against him. He caught her face in his hands and she did not resist when he lift her chin toward him, didn't move away when he put his mouth on hers.

She parted her lips and invited him in, and with a small groan, Lance pressed it all into memory. The slide of her tongue, the smell of her shampoo, the soft cotton sweater she wore and the way her arms felt below it. He memorized the soft, tiny sound she made, both protest and yearning, and it was, at last, the reason he let her go.

Because he couldn't stand the thought of hurting her. And if he let her go now, he never would. With a halfhearted smile, he touched her cheek. "I wish I were another kind of man, Tamara. You're a hell of a woman."

And then, before he could change his mind, he left her.

Chapter Fifteen

Lance walked home through the snow, his mind whirling. But once there, he couldn't light, couldn't think. He needed someone to talk to.

And without really knowing why he picked him, Lance went looking for his brother Jake. Lord knew Jake had a lot of problems of his own at the moment, but all Lance needed was a sounding board, someone to listen to him talk it all through. Of anyone, Jake was also most likely to understand.

There was too much snow to even consider getting out his car, but the condo Jake rented wasn't far, so Lance set out on foot again, walking through the silent, pristine streets, taking pleasure in the snow still drifting from a dark sky.

Home. Man, he'd missed it.

Jake's place was located in an upscale development

with good access to the ski roads. Most of them were time shares, or vacation homes of the wealthy, and there were more gorgeous, well-tended women in the five-acre square than anyplace outside Hollywood. Lance rang the bell to his brother's apartment, admiring the very fine assets of a girl in tight pants as she cleaned off her car.

But that was all he did—admire. Another Lance, another time, might have leaned over the railing and whistled at her. More likely he'd have called out and started a flirtation that would end up in an exchange of phone numbers.

Today, it didn't seem that interesting. A nice rear end wasn't much to go on, after all. And this one wasn't nearly as nice as Tamara's, even if she didn't show it off like this.

He heard his thoughts with a sense of annoyance, and pushed the bell again, more impatiently. You'd think he'd never slept with a woman before the way he kept going over last night in his head.

Jake flung open the door, bleary-eyed and unshaved. "Lance!" He shoved his thick black hair off his forehead. "What the hell are you doing here?"

"Nice welcome. A brother can't drop by?"

Jake crossed his arms over his bare chest, shivering in a pair of sweats. "Well, he could, but this one never does. Come on in."

The apartment, for all its built-in luxury, was even worse than Lance's. Lance's was at least neat. Jake's furniture was covered with discarded clothes, and an empty wine bottle with two glasses littered the coffee table.

Seeing the evidence, Lance said, "You have a

woman here? Maybe I should come back another time.''

Jake moved into the kitchen and began to measure coffee into the basket. ''There's always a woman here. No big deal.''

Something about the comment brought Tamara to mind. How hurt she would be if Lance said that about her. ''I guess it hasn't occurred to you that maybe those women have feelings, huh?''

''Look who's talking. I'm not the one who got a black eye from a jilted lover the first day back in town.''

Lance didn't particularly want to think about that. ''One time. Big deal.''

Jake snorted. ''C'mon, Lance. This is a case of the pot calling the kettle black, and you know it.'' He shook his hair out of his face. ''It's not like I'm going around with the girl next door. I'm just another notch on their belts.''

The girl next door.

Lance rubbed his stomach restlessly. That was the problem, wasn't it? There were rules, and Lance had broken all of them by going after Tamara. It made him feel vaguely ill.

''Just be careful,'' he said.

Jake leaned a hip on the kitchen counter. His eyes were almost a neon blue, all the more startling against the darkness of his hair. The hollows that had made him look gaunt at the Wild Moose a few weeks earlier seemed even worse. ''Did you come here to give me a lecture on sex in the nineties?''

''No.'' He narrowed his eyes. ''You look like hell, though. Are you still not sleeping?''

For a single moment, Jake closed his eyes. It made him look unbearably weary. "It's not so much the sleep, but the dreams."

"Why don't you get some help, man?"

Jake shook his head. "I'm fine."

Yeah. In a pig's eye. Jake had suffered more at the hands of their father than either of his brothers had. Somewhere along the line, he'd internalized Olan's driving, perfectionist standards. It was killing him now.

As if he knew how he looked, Jake straightened suddenly and tossed his hair out of his eyes. "What's up? You look like you've got something on your mind."

Lance remembered why he had come. "I have something to tell you."

"Shoot." He stretched across the counter and snagged a ruby-colored terry cloth robe.

"Well, there's no easy way to it, so I'll just say it. I found out that Valerie had a baby—my baby—before she died. Her cousin has been raising him all this time."

"Is that the bartender at the Wild Moose, the one you were so hot for?"

Annoyance rose in Lance's chest. "I wasn't hot for her, but that's the one."

"And she laid this story on you and you just believed her? That her kid is really her cousin's, and you're the father?" He took a mug from the mess on the counter and rinsed it out. "Haven't you learned anything?"

Lance tried to remind himself that his brother was

burned-out and near the end of his rope, but it didn't help. "Tamara wouldn't lie."

"Is that right?" Jake lifted a dark, arched brow. "All women lie, little brother."

"You don't know her."

"I don't have to. I know her kind."

Lance narrowed his eyes. "Not all women are like your wife, you know. And not all women are like Valerie."

"Uh-huh. What makes this one so different?"

"She has no reason to lie." Which wasn't quite true. She was poor as the proverbial church mouse, and stood to gain a lot financially if Lance took her on. But stubbornly, he said, "She has integrity, Jake. She's so good with him, too. You should see her with that boy—and he's not even her blood child. She's given up everything to take care of him, and that makes me feel like hell."

Jake looked at him. "You've got it bad, don't you?"

"What?"

"Poor bastard." Jake shook his head. "I've never seen you like this."

"It's not like that," Jake said. "I have a lot of respect for her. She's not like Valerie, if that's what you mean."

"I didn't say she was. You had it bad for Valerie, but that wasn't your heart talking, if you get my drift." He sipped his coffee lazily, his neon eyes glowing with that eerie, near madness. "At least get a blood test. Make sure the boy is really yours."

It was a reasonable expectation, especially considering Valerie had never exactly been known for her faithfulness. But Lance saw Tamara's green eyes, so guileless and wary, and he didn't want to see the expression that would be there when he made that request. "No."

Jake inclined his head, and for one moment, Lance caught a glimpse of the old Jake. "She must really be something."

A deep stabbing ache ripped through his chest. "She is that," he said, and his voice sounded rough. And more quietly, "She is that."

Jake moved abruptly, putting his cup down. "I'd give half my life to feel a glimmering of faith in a woman right now." His jaw looked hard. "Don't let her get away."

Lance laughed bitterly. "But don't you see, Jake? It's practically a criminal act for a Forrest to settle in with a woman that good."

"Yeah." He picked up his cup again. "But I'd still get a blood test. Don't be a fool."

But Lance didn't do it. He didn't have to—he only had to look at Cody to see the extraordinary family resemblance. And the bottom line was, he trusted Tamara. He also knew he'd been with Valerie nearly every waking minute through that three-week period at Christmas all those years ago. She wouldn't have had time to have another lover.

Cody was his. And damn anyone who said differently.

He tried not to consider the possibility that he wanted to believe it because he wanted an excuse to make Tamara's life easier.

Over the next few days, Lance occupied himself

with the details of this big change in his life. He spoke
to his accountant, and had him draw up a monthly
payment schedule that was double the state standard.
He'd have made it triple, but doubted Tamara would
accept it.

He also made arrangements for a single lump sum
to be paid for back child support the day she signed
the papers granting him visitation rights. He thought
that was enough to ask for in the beginning.

The one stipulation he asked for, and Tamara
agreed, much to his relief, was that neither of them
could take Cody out of Red Creek. Lance wanted the
stability of the small town for Cody, but he also worried that Tamara might, since she would have the fi-
nancial wherewithal, return to the university.

It made him feel like a heel in some ways—of all
things, the university life was one she'd aspired toward
for many years—but he couldn't bear the idea that
he'd finally come to know his son, and then she'd
marry someone else and leave Red Creek.

He told his mother. She was not surprised—she'd
suspected Cody was Lance's child, but hadn't realized
he "started up again with that Valerie," as she put it.
Tyler was as pleased as he ever was about anything,
and said it would make Curtis happy to have a cousin.

Jake didn't say anything else about the blood test.

After a week, Lance was finally ready to face Cody
himself. Saturday morning dawned bright and crisp,
with a promise of more Indian summer in the air. The
snow, except in shady spots, was gone, and Lance
woke up with the taste of trout in his mouth.

He called Tamara. It was harder than he thought to
hear her voice. The sound of it sent a wave of need

through him, deep and wide, and for a moment, he sat on the other end of the line, seized by an erotic vision of her in the car, half-naked as they drove through Red Creek.

"Is anyone there?" she repeated.

"Sorry," he said. "It's Lance."

A short pause. "I recognize your voice, you know."

"Oh." On a pad of paper, he drew an almond-shaped eye. "I just wondered if I could come get Cody this morning for a few hours, and take him fishing at the lake." He cleared his scratchy throat. "I thought maybe it was time to get going on all this. Make it right."

"I see." She sounded afraid.

"Tamara, I'm serious about what I said at the lawyer's office." They'd met there briefly two days before to go over the details. He'd seen the immense relief on her face when she heard his custody request—simple visitation, nothing more. And although she'd protested the amount of money he wanted to settle upon them, he'd managed to talk her around. "I'm not going to interfere."

"I know. It's just strange." She paused, and in the silence, Lance could hear Mozart playing in the background. "The truth is, I usually spend Saturdays with him, and I'll miss that."

"We can do it tomorrow, if you'd rather. Or I can baby-sit when you need to work. Just tell me what works best for you."

"No, today is fine," she said. "I have a test on Monday and I need to study."

"Are you sure?" The eye he was sketching took on an elliptical fold, that distinctly American Indian and

Asian detail that gave Tamara's eyes such an exotic cast. "Tomorrow is supposed to be really gorgeous, too. We can fish then, instead."

"No, I think he'd love to go today. I'll get him ready."

To make things as easy as possible for both of them, Lance tried to make it short when he came to pick up an eager Cody, who was practically bursting with the anticipation of a fishing trip. His exuberance took some of the strain out of the air, but Lance still couldn't look at Tamara head on, and he noticed she kept her distance.

"Don't let him fall in the lake," she said.

"I won't."

"Cody, you mind, you hear? When you go by a lake, you have to behave yourself."

"Or you can get drownded."

"Drowned. Right." She buttoned his jacket and kissed his forehead. "Have fun."

For a split second, Lance caught her gaze. For that single heartbeat, a flare of pure yearning and silent agreement passed between them. Then it was gone. "C'mon, kiddo. Let's go catch us some trout for supper."

Tamara watched them through the big front window with a sense of deep loss. Lance took Cody's hand, and they walked to his car, two blond heads shining in the sun, two loping walks. Father and son.

And she didn't even have the comfort of being Cody's mother, of being part of the union that had created this beautiful child. It made her feel alienated, like she'd never really belonged in the picture. Now Cody would take his rightful place among the Forrest family, while Tamara was only his caretaker, with nothing to give him.

It was a lot more depressing than she would have expected. Hadn't she wanted this for Cody? With the money Lance provided for his care, Tamara would be able to at last afford some of the things she'd longed to give him and simply couldn't: a computer to help stimulate his astounding mind before he got bored, art and dance classes if he wanted them, a musical instrument a little later. She would be able to afford to buy him many books, and wouldn't have to worry about the price of peewee football uniforms.

All the things she'd had to do without as a child. All the things she'd been desperately afraid Cody would have to do without.

And she couldn't ask for an arrangement that was any fairer, or with a better man. Lance had shouldered his responsibility easily, fairly, quickly, without undue demands or restrictions. He had the power to do anything he wished, and he had only asked for simple visitation privileges.

So why was she so unhappy this morning?

Lance.

It was Lance. Somehow, his arrival in Red Creek had turned her whole life upside down. What had seemed normal in the past was now intolerable. His vividness, the bold brightness he'd brought into her life, made everything that went before seem drab and gray.

Because it *had* been drab and gray.

Now Tamara found herself filled with yearning, the

normal yearnings of a young woman. She wanted to make love more than once every four years. She wanted a husband to share her life with, more children, a job she cared about and that felt important, not just something to pay the rent.

And even more. She wanted a life filled with books and music and stimulating conversation, a real life, not the grinding day-to-day struggle that had marked her own mother's life.

Slowly Tamara looked around the room, feeling a dawning sense of awareness. Her mother had loved her with a deep, devoted passion, but the struggle had put her in an early grave. Would her mother have succumbed to a disease like cancer so young if her life had been smoother? If she'd had a husband to help her? If she hadn't had to struggle so hard every single day?

Maybe she would have anyway. Disease was capricious and unfair. But Tamara couldn't help thinking that life had worn her mother down so much that when the cancer struck she had no reserves left with which to fight it.

Surprised, tears sprung to her eyes. "Oh, Mama, what would you tell me now? What should I do?"

And suddenly Tamara knew. Her mother would say the same things she always had: don't settle for anything less than exactly what you want. Fight as hard as you can. Don't ever give up.

For four long years, Tamara had been lost. In retrospect, she saw that she'd been grieving her mother deeply when everything with Valerie happened. That grief, and the unexpected desertion by Eric, had clouded her judgment. She could have gone back to finish her degree, but she'd been too overwhelmed. It was just easier to stay in Red Creek with Cody. In Red Creek where things were familiar, where her mother lingered in the breath of the trees and the sun on the mountains; and in the aisles of the grocery stores.

And here in Red Creek, she had fallen into a rut, a rut of survival that echoed her mother's life with Tamara. It was an odd tribute, and not surprising, but it was also not at all what her mother would have wanted for her. Her mother had made the monumental effort to move a thousand miles from home to give Tamara a better life than the one she'd known.

And in her rut Tamara might have stayed forever if not for the bold, blindingly bright presence of Lance Forrest, blowing into town like a carnival, exciting and full of laughter.

Smiling, Tamara thought he was also as inconstant as a carnival, but there was nothing wrong with that. It wasn't a quality a woman wanted in a husband, but he never made any pretenses about that.

Which made it possible to love him as he was.

If she were truly honest, she had to admit she also wanted Lance Forrest. Part of her discontent this morning had to do with the fact that she wanted more than breath to have gone with them to the lake. Just to hear him laugh. Just to see that glittering mischief in his eyes. Just to touch his strong forearm one more time.

"No," she said aloud. The facts were, he wasn't husband material and she wouldn't try to make him so. There were things you couldn't do to a person. He was as free as a hawk in the sky. It would be cruel to cage him.

With bittersweet resignation, she knew she would get over him. Someday.

In the meantime, she would accept the gift he'd brought into her life. She would break this dull routine. She would claim the life she wanted.

On the table were her loathed accounting books. Very slowly Tamara smiled.

No more accounting, not another single minute. She didn't care if it messed up her grade-point average. She loved history and poetry and literature, and she intended to spend her life immersed in them, teaching or researching or whatever she could find. There was no law that said she had to spend her life at a university. She was only a few credits away from her degree. She could make arrangements to study three days a week in Denver to complete them, especially now that she knew Cody had family in town.

Then she could teach. At the high school or the junior high, or even at the community college. They went through teachers like spring snowfall in this climate—people always thought living in the mountains would be glamorous and thrilling, but the reality was, the winters chased a good many of them away within a year.

Feeling exhilarated, Tamara slammed her accounting books closed, picked them up and put them in the trash. As she did it, she laughed.

And inexplicably, found herself in tears at the rush of emotion in her breast. "Oh, Lance," she whispered. "Why can't you be the marrying kind?"

Chapter Sixteen

On the shores of Lake Rosalie, Lance taught Cody to fish. The weather was as gorgeous as he had anticipated, well into the fifties by noon. Coupled with the high-altitude sunlight, fierce even at midwinter, they were warm enough to shed their jackets before long, and Lance worried that Cody's fair skin might burn. Lance found a baseball cap in his trunk and popped it on Cody's head.

And all morning, Lance thought about his own father. When the two of them had come out here, Olan became a different man—patient, kind, quiet. In all the times they'd gone fishing together, Olan had only lost his infamous temper once, when Lance fell out of the rowboat and nearly drowned because he'd been showing off.

The memories made him miss Olan deeply. "You

know," he said to Cody, "my daddy used to bring me out here sometimes. He taught me to fish, just like I'm teaching you."

"He did? How come he doesn't fish with you now?"

"Well, he was old," Lance said, even though he hadn't been. Not really. "He died a couple of months ago."

Cody looked up at him solemnly. "Are you sad?"

"Yeah, I am sometimes." Lance felt a tug on his line. "Hey, I think I got something."

He reeled in a little, and sure enough, the fierce weight of a fish tugged back. "Hold on, Cody. We got us a live one." It might be a big one, too, by the feel of it. Lance carefully reeled in a little, then let it fight and pull out the line, feeling the quick, familiar excitement of a fighting fish on his line. His mouth filled with the anticipation of lemon-drenched rainbow trout.

And beside him, Cody was filled with questions. Why didn't he pull the fish out of the water? Why did the fish fight? Would the fish die?

Tough questions, but Lance believed in the honor of fishing. He had respect for the creatures, and respected their fight, but he had also grown up on fresh-caught trout. It was a lot more honorable, at least in his view, to come out here and face the fish himself than let somebody else butcher it for him.

Holding carefully to his pole, he knelt next to Cody and helped the boy close his hands around the pole. "Feel that tugging?" he said.

"Yeah."

"Now we're going to bring him in." Slowly he

reeled the trout, letting Cody help him turn the reel, feeling by the fight and tension on the line that it was going to be an admirable fish indeed.

When at last Lance felt the fish near the surface of the lake, he gently took the reel from Cody's hands and said, "Watch this. He's gonna come out of that water and be more beautiful than anything you ever saw."

With impeccable timing, Lance tugged—and the trout came flapping out of the water, suspended for a moment against the sunlight, silver and flashing and furiously fighting. In exhilaration, Lance whooped. The fish landed on shore. Mercifully, he hit his head on a rock and lay still immediately. Lance knelt and put his hand on the cold fish. He looked at Cody, whose bright blue eyes looked uncertain. "One thing you can do, if you want," Lance said, "is to tell the fish thank you for giving his life to feed you."

He waited. Cody finally knelt with fierce concentration. "Thank you," he said, patting the trout's silver body.

And there in the clean, crisp morning, with a ten-pound trout at his feet and a beautiful, sweet little boy at his side, Lance was struck with a fierce, all-encompassing sense of fatherhood. The emotion was so deep, Lance almost could not breathe. Love, uncomplicated and clean and somehow healing, filled him like soda in a glass, effervescent and foaming.

"Good work, kid."

Cody beamed at him. "What do we do with him now?"

"We'll put him in this bucket over here, and then

we'll take him home and cook him for supper. You ever had trout baked with lemon?''

"No."

"Mmm. You'll love it."

"I'm hungry."

Lance chuckled. "Well, we have to wait on the fish, but I did bring some sandwiches and cookies. How about that?"

"Okay."

They sat on the rocky shores of the lake, looking out at the water. Lance was surprised by the length of Cody's attention span. He didn't seem to need to rush and run, just sat quietly eating peanut butter and jelly. Lance was used to Curtis, who couldn't sit still for three minutes.

And finally, it felt like the right moment to tell him. Lance had been worrying about it all day, but now his mouth just opened and he said, "Cody, what if I told you I'm your dad?"

Cody looked up. "I don't have a dad."

"Well, yes you do." Lance lifted his eyebrows. "I'm your dad."

"But I don't have a dad," he said again, a frown tugging his brows down thunderously. "I only have a mom."

This wasn't going the way he'd expected. "You haven't had one until now," he said. "But that's because I didn't know you were my little boy until now. I would have come sooner if I'd known."

"You're my dad?" Cody said in a little voice.

"Yeah. Is that okay with you?"

Cody took a bite of his sandwich and looked at the lake for a long minute. Or maybe it only felt long because Lance was afraid he'd screwed everything up. At last, Cody said, "Curtis has a dad, but he doesn't have a mother."

"I know. You know what? Curtis's dad is your uncle Tyler." He smiled. "And Curtis's grandmother is your grandmother."

That got his attention. A blaze of joy covered the little boy's face. "My *real* grandma?"

Lance chuckled. Mothers were good. Dads were okay, but grandmas were the ultimate. "Yep."

Cody leapt up and gave Lance a huge, encompassing hug. "Oh, boy! I love my grandma!"

Lance closed his eyes, smelling peanut butter and sunshine on the soft, round little body of his son. He felt almost dizzy with love. "She loves you, too, kiddo. Let's go ask your mom if you can go see your grandma now."

Cody pulled back and nodded vigorously. Before Lance entirely let him go, Cody put his small hand on Lance's cheek. "You're my daddy?"

"Yes."

"Can I call you Daddy?"

Lance found his throat didn't work. He nodded.

Life changed with blinding speed for Tamara over the next few weeks. Money and time—the two most strained commodities in her life for four years—were suddenly plentiful. Besides, for Lance's generous sum for back child support, between Ty and Curtis, Louise, and Lance himself, Tamara found she never had to worry about finding a baby-sitter.

With the money, she was cautious. She invested most of it in a high-yield savings account. She bought

Cody new clothes, and herself a new pair of jeans. And one Saturday morning, right after Lance came to pick up Cody, she went to Denver for the day. She brought home two things, a modest but powerful computer setup, and a winter catalog for the University of Colorado at Denver.

The boxes were still sitting in the living room when Lance brought Cody home. She was cooking supper when they came in, chattering about trucks, and Tamara gathered they'd been to the warehouse where Forrest Construction kept their heavy equipment.

"Mom!" Cody cried, running into the kitchen. "I got to ride in a tractor!"

"Good for you," she said, and kissed him. "Are you about ready to eat?"

"I'm starving!"

"Good. Go wash your hands and get ready."

He ran off. Tamara heard Lance in the living room, grunting over the computer, but she felt oddly frozen at the stove, her hand permanently attached to the wooden spoon in her hand.

Three weeks, and not one night had passed that Tamara didn't stay awake long after she should have been sleeping, thinking of Lance in her bed. Her pillows smelled of his hair, and the mattress held the notes of his skin. It was probably her imagination, but it felt real enough. She couldn't climb under the covers without remembering the searing night they'd spent together there. She thought often that it would be easier to just sleep on the couch.

Instead, she somehow slept there again and again, sinfully spinning erotic pictures of his mouth on her neck, his hands gliding over her body. Over and over again, she thought of him coming into the kitchen that morning, and planting that single kiss on her mouth.

The vivid imaginings spilled over into her waking life, making it hard to look Lance in the eye when he came to get Cody, or dropped him off. She was afraid he'd see the longing in her eyes. It would be humiliating beyond words.

Because he seemed to accept this new, platonic relationship without any trouble. He was polite and distant, in order to give her dignity, she supposed. One night, when she was coming home from work, she'd seen him in his car with a laughing brunette, very elegant and slim. Obviously out on a date.

She tried not to think about it.

Tonight he was lingering longer than usual. Generally, he simply walked Cody to the door, came in for a moment and left again. She wondered what was keeping him tonight.

The computer. Of course. Maybe he might even know how to set it up. Putting the spoon down, she hurried into the other room.

But coming onto him suddenly was not a good idea. He knelt before the boxes, one strong hand on the computer box. His coat was shed carelessly on the couch, and the sleeve of his shirt was rolled three quarters of the way up, showing that beautiful, vein-ridged forearm. His hair had still not been cut since his return, and it was starting to spill over his shoulders the smallest bit, thick and golden and touchable.

A wave of such violent desire struck her that Tamara couldn't remember what had brought her into the room. She stopped in the archway, breathless with want.

He looked up, and for one wishful moment, Tamara thought she saw the same hunger in his eyes. It disappeared in an instant, replaced by a smile that held not a trace of guile or seduction. "You got a computer. Good move."

His voice, sounding so normal, broke the heated spell. Tamara lifted her eyebrows ruefully. "It seemed like a great idea at the time, but you know me and machines—now I'm afraid to set it up."

"Well, ma'am, it just so happens that I know a little about it. Would you like me to do it for you?"

No. Yes. Both answers rose in her mind. If she said okay, she'd have to endure his company for much longer than she thought she could bear it. If she said no, the computer might sit in its boxes for weeks while she developed enough nerve to tackle it.

She couldn't decide.

Lance carefully put the instruction booklet aside. "I guess you'd like a little time alone with Cody, huh? I understand." He rose and reached for his coat.

"No. I mean, that's not it." She felt an embarrassing blush rise in her face. "I would like your help, but I'm reluctant to ask anything more of you." She lifted a shoulder. "You've been so kind already."

"Well, how about a trade?" He cocked his head. "You feed me some of that supper that smells so good, and I'll set up the computer right afterward."

"It's just spaghetti," she said. "But you're more than welcome."

"Just spaghetti," he echoed. "Sounds excellent. I'm so sick of canned green chili I could die."

"Canned green chili? Yuck."

He shrugged. "Exactly. I'm dying for home-cooked

food, and unfortunately, my mother will not take pity on me every single night. I'm only allowed once or twice a week." He gave her his dazzling grin. "She says I'm plenty old enough to have learned to cook for myself."

Tamara chuckled, her nervousness easing with the conversation. "She's right."

"I can cook. It's just boring to cook for yourself. You ever notice that?"

There was a hint of loneliness in his words, and Tamara was suddenly glad to be able to provide something small to ease it. "Come on. We'll eat in the kitchen."

Lance couldn't take his eyes off of her. Tonight she wore a dark green sweater that had seen better days. He liked the way the old threads shaped themselves to her body, cupping her breasts, molding her gorgeous rear end, even giving him a glimpse of soft white breast peeking over the V neck every now and then. Instead of her usual jeans, she wore a simple full skirt, warm and long, with socks on her feet. It made her look feminine and sweet.

As they ate, his wretched imagination kept giving him alluring visions of the body below that sweater, of those jade-green eyes heated to twice their intensity when she was filled with desire and him. He kept imagining the way it would feel to kiss her, slip his hand inside her sweater, make her cry out again. He kept remembering how responsive she was, so richly accepting of her body's demands that she had come apart against him.

He wanted to do it again.

But he kept his conversation light, telling jokes about the job they were doing for a fussy suburbanite who'd changed her mind about the position of light fixtures three times. He played straight man to Cody's knock-knock jokes. Tamara laughed easily, and filled his plate twice, and seemed completely unaware of the effect she had on him. It drove him crazy.

Cody, worn-out after the long day, was cranky through most of the meal, and Tamara picked him up firmly after he'd drank a cup of milk. "I think someone needs an early bedtime," she said to Lance. "If you want to get started on the computer, I'll be back in a few minutes."

Lance stood up, smiling, and bent close to kiss Cody's cheek. He did it partly for Cody, but partly to get close to Tamara, as well, close enough he sensed her warmth. Close enough her hair brushed his cheek. Close enough he found himself instantly, painfully hard.

"Night," he said.

"Night, Daddy," Cody replied, laying his head on his mother's shoulder. Lance turned away, hiding himself behind the table. Maybe she wouldn't notice. But maybe she would.

"I'll be back in a minute," she said. Her voice was perfectly even.

He scraped and stacked the plates and wiped off the stove and counter. He wouldn't take the time to do the dishes because it was going to be tough enough to get out of here without making an idiot of himself as it was. She'd made it perfectly plain she didn't want him—that he wasn't her kind of man, and Lance had enough sense to know it was true. He'd get the computer together and get the hell out of here.

By the time she returned, he'd opened all the boxes and taken the components out, examining each one for any sign of trouble or tampering. It was a good machine—not fancy, but very good. When she returned, he said as much. "You must have done your homework."

"Actually, I don't know very much about it." She sat in a chair by the lamp and tucked a lock of hair behind her ear. "The guy in the store was very helpful. He even gave me a fifteen percent discount on the price."

Lightly, to fight the rise of jealousy he felt, Lance said, "Must have thought you were cute." He looked up to gauge her reaction.

She smiled, and it was a very womanly, knowing smile. "I think you could be right."

Lance fought the wild, dark emotion that rose in him at the thought of some other man with his hands on her. He tried to summon a devilish comment or wicked smile, but they both deserted him. "Well, I'm glad you got a good deal." He shifted his gaze from her eyes and halted.

The sweater she wore was made of some kind of open weave, with little holes that didn't mean much—until the light was behind her. As it was now.

It illuminated everything, coming from behind to highlight one breast perfectly under the loose fabric. He felt electrified as he absorbed the simple beauty of the light touching her that way, washing down her slim side, curving around her ribs, kissing the edge of a nipple. A nipple, he noticed with a wave of dizziness, that was unmistakably aroused.

He looked up. Before she could hide it, he saw a naked yearning on her face, an expression of such furious hunger that it knocked the wind out of him. Slowly he put down the instruction packet in his hands.

Deliberately this time, he let her see him look at her—at her face, at her beautiful, seductive mouth, at her throat and at her breasts. She didn't move, and the air was so thick with the promise of their passion that Lance felt dizzy. "You know," he said quietly, "the light comes right through that sweater. I can see your breasts like you were naked."

He almost didn't hear her, she spoke so quietly. "I know."

She'd done it on purpose. Sat in that chair knowing he would see her body and be tempted. The thought shattered his control. He stood up and walked to the chair, not caring that she might be able to tell this time that he was aroused. He dropped to his knees before the chair, and reached for her.

At the first brush of his hand over her shoulder, Tamara made a pained sound, and he lost it. He pulled her close, tugging her legs around him. She came willingly, wrapping herself around him, pressing her body close to his. His hands fell almost savagely in her hair and he hauled her to him, plunging his tongue in her mouth with a groan. That sweet mouth, so eager and hungry and deep.

But not enough. He felt blind and deaf and dumb, aware only of the violent need of a woman he could not get out of his head. He reached for the edge of her sweater and pulled, frustrated that he could not get it off quickly enough. It stuck on her shoulders, and he bent his head to kiss that creamy flesh, following her collarbone to the hollow of her throat, struggling to free her from the sweater.

All at once, it tore with a sound that seemed very loud. Tamara cried out, pulling him closer, and with a cry, he tore harder. It tumbled off her shoulders, catching at her elbows. Lance unfastened the bra below, freeing her breasts to his mouth, to his hands. Her skin was silky, supple, warm, and he felt he would explode. He thought he'd imagined how she felt, that no one could be so beautiful to the eye and to the touch and to the taste. But she was. He sucked her deeply into his mouth, kneading her hips with his hands, feeling her fingers digging into his flesh.

And this time, he wouldn't lose her. Not this time. He reached below her skirts and yanked off her panties, and freed himself, and there, kneeling before her, her torn sweater falling around her beautiful breasts and graceful shoulders, Lance entered her with one sure, clean stroke.

Like the rest, this was violent. She moved to accommodate him, clinging to his shoulders, her legs clasped around him. Her skirt draped his thighs, and he clutched her thighs as his need rose to a wild screaming in him. Her name rose to his lips like a chant, like a lifeline, and he whispered it softly, over and over, his heart pounding with need and love and hunger and a thousand things he couldn't name. He felt whole for the first time since he'd been in her bed, whole like uncut bread, like sunlight.

He came apart against her, even as he tried to resist.

She clutched him tight and Lance shuddered, aching to cry out, knowing he couldn't or he'd wake Cody. In a mindless, thoughtless, light-struck plane, he gave her himself on a level he knew he'd never given.

She held out almost to the last instant, and then Lance felt her follow him, the spasms of her body wrenching around him, giving him the last possible heights of pleasure. She held him tight, arms and legs and body, and buried her face in his hair, making a quiet aching sound that stabbed clear through him, her hands dug deep in his hair.

When it was spent, they did not separate. Lance sunk onto his knees, holding her close to him, kissing her shoulder, stroking her back, smelling her deep. She let herself be held.

"You feel so good," he said, and his voice was hoarse. "I've wanted you every minute of every day since the last time."

"Me, too," she confessed against his neck. She straightened to look at him, their bodies still joined. "You must think I'm a terrible hussy."

"No." The tattered sweater, revealing her nakedness, was almost unbearably erotic. He opened a palm on her shoulder and stroked her skin, the upper slope of her breast, her arm. "No," he repeated. "You're passionate and sexy and beautiful. Good things." He circled the tip of her breast with one finger. "You make me crazy, Tamara. I'm not kidding."

"I used to have a boyfriend," she said, tracing the edge of the hair on his chest, "who hated it when I did something like that to try and seduce him." She looked at him, suddenly earnest. "I should be ashamed, but I couldn't stand for you to leave tonight without—'' She halted, stricken.

He kissed her urgently. ''Don't ever be ashamed with me. Not ever.'' He clasped her face between his hands and kissed her again, very gently. He closed his eyes to concentrate on just the sweetness of her mouth, and a thickness filled his throat. He wanted to protect her, to please her, take care of her. ''I think that man must have been an idiot.''

''I think he was.''

Now came the awkward part. They were both half-undressed and somehow there had to be some dignity to recomposing themselves. His legs were falling asleep. Gently he reached for the blanket on the chair, and pulled it forward to drape around her shoulders. ''I must be getting old,'' he said with a smile. ''We have to move before I can't walk tomorrow.''

She clutched the blanket around her shoulders, and with a small sound, eased away. Her skirts fluttered down modestly, and the blanket covered her as she sat on the floor. Lance shifted and pulled his clothes back together, but when she would have moved away completely, he grabbed her. Settling in the chair, he tugged her hand, intending to cradle her in his lap for a while.

Suddenly she went rigid. ''Lance,'' she said, horror on her face. ''We didn't use a condom.''

A cold wash of claustrophobia struck him. He'd never, ever forgotten such a thing before. What the hell was wrong with him?

But he had a sick feeling that he knew.

The wild man of Red Creek, with a string of women from here to Timbuktu, had fallen in love, fallen in love with a woman he could not allow himself to want.

Jake had been right, that snowy cold morning. Lance had it bad. And instead of falling for someone like himself, someone with a wild streak who might forgive the odd night lost to drink or wanderlust or any number of sins, Lance had lost his head over a woman who needed to be safe and secure and steady. All the things he wasn't.

Chapter Seventeen

Tamara lay within the circle of Lance's embrace and tried to ignore the war of emotions in her breast. Her head fit exactly into the cradle of his shoulder, and his arms fit comfortably around her. So right. He was so right.

Even this moment, which could have been awkward and strange, was not. They curled together in the chair without speaking, a warmth and comfortable silence pulsing between them, a silence that needed no artificial bracing.

Under her ear, Tamara could hear his heart beating, a dear and intimate sound. Hearing it, Tamara put her hand over the place, on his silky-haired chest, and wanted to tell him that she loved him. She wanted to tell him she loved the gentleness of his hand in her hair now, in contrast to the hungry violence of their joining. She wanted to tell him that the scent of his skin in her nose was like all the best of a mountain summer, like a meadow at noon. She wanted to tell him he was the most generous,. kind man she'd ever known.

But her confession would burden him, and instead, she simply turned her face to his chest and nuzzled him.

His embrace tightened, and under her ear, his heart moved faster. She wondered what he would say if he could find the courage. She wondered if he felt the same strange comfort with her that she did with him.

"I'm sorry about that, Tamara," he said into the quiet.

"About what?"

"About the condom. It never even crossed my mind." His hand slid up and down her back, kneading and circling. "You won't get sick or anything—I swear. I got tested a couple of months ago for a physical, and you're the only woman I've slept with in six or eight months."

Six or eight months? "Careful," she said with a private smile, "someone might figure out you aren't the wild man you used to be."

He chuckled. "Yeah, well, we all get older."

"It isn't disease I'm worried about, exactly," she said, still not moving.

"Don' t worry about the other. I'd take care of you. You know that."

Not *I'd marry you and we'll raise our child,* but *I'd take care of you.* "I know."

Much as she regretted it, that single sentence changed the mood between them. It grew strained, filled with unspoken wishes, unsaid promises, unvoiced thoughts. She didn't want the future or the past to come between them right now, but they did. She pushed against him and sat up. "I guess I'd better get something decent on."

He made no protest. Only nodded and looked at his watch, as if nothing at all had passed between them. "Jake's decided to buy a restaurant—The Wild Moose—and I'm supposed to meet him there in a little while to discuss some remodeling. Maybe I can come back and finish the computer for you tomorrow."

"Sure ." Tamara clutched the blanket more closely around her body. "That's fine."

He must have sensed her sudden stiffness. He sat up, moving her on his lap. "Look at me, Tamara." Once again, he had to nudge her chin to overcome her reluctance to look at him.

It was just so hard to look at him head-on like that. Hard to bear the full brunt of his shining goldenness and feel the emotions his face struck to life in her.

But she did it, lifted her eyes to his. A snippet of a poem rushed into her mind, and she spoke it softly, "'Tyger! Tyger! burning bright. / In the forests of the night.'"

"Am I a tiger, Tamara?"

"No," she said, and found herself smiling as she lifted a hand to smooth his thick hair from his forehead. Such a broad, intelligent brow. "You just make me think of that beauty."

He looked stricken at her words. "No one has ever said anything like that to me before." He plucked her hand from her lap and kissed it. "You're so different from any woman I've ever met. I want you know that."

Dread welled in her. "Why?"

"Because...this is..." He scowled, his attention focused on her hand, on the fingers he stroked. "We can't do this again. We can't. I'm not the right man for you, and you need to be free to find him. I don't want to screw anything up for you."

"Lance, you don't owe me anything. I'm a grown woman. I can fend for myself, make my own decisions."

At last he looked at her, his blue eyes full of regret. "I owe you a lot."

And all at once, Tamara felt a fierce certainty that she needed to tell him what she thought, what she felt. It might be her only chance, and if life had taught her anything, the simple fact that people weren't always there the next day was primary. "If I were given the choice of all the men in the world to choose from," she said quietly, "no one in the world would have a chance next to you, Lance."

He started to speak. She raised a hand to his mouth. "Shh. I know you aren't the marrying kind, but you're a good man."

"Tamara, don't. I can't—"

"You don't understand," she said with a smile. "I think very well of myself. I don't give myself away. I don't think very highly of the morals and attitudes of most of the men on the planet. I wish you could see yourself through my eyes, that you could see what I see when I look at you."

He swallowed. "I wish I could, too."

Taking a breath, she smiled. "Don't ever think you're a bad man because you're honest enough to be who you are."

Then, before he could react, she stood up. "It's probably time for you to go home."

For a minute, he didn't move. Then he stood up, kissed her lightly and moved toward his jacket. There was a curious stiffness in his movements that contrasted sharply with his usual long-limbed grace. He paused at the door. "If I were another kind of man, I'd have married you the second time I met you."

Tamara bowed her head at the longing that gave her. When she looked up again, he was closing the front door behind him. And this time, he was truly gone.

For days, Lance moved through his life in a dark cocoon. He snapped at employees, broke the dates his brother had made for him and snarled at everyone who got in his path. His mother told him not to come back to visit until he had a better attitude. His secretary tiptoed in and out of his office without a word. If he had had a dog, it would have been cowering in the corner.

Friday night was the dance at the country club to which he'd promised to escort Marissa. As he donned his good Italian suit he wished fervently he could avoid the whole thing. But a promise was a promise, and whatever else anybody said about him, he kept his word.

To his surprise, just seeing Marissa's calm, luminescent face eased something in him. "I feel compelled to warn you," he said as she got in the car, "that wild boars have been fleeing my path lately."

She grinned. "Bad mood, huh?"

"That's putting it mildly." He kissed her cheek. "You look especially nice tonight. I like that color on you."

"Thanks." She smoothed the ruby-colored fabric over her thighs. "My mother always told me I should never wear pastels. Turns out she was right about one thing, anyway.''

The sound of a motorcycle broke the night, and a chopped, gleaming Harley growled into Marissa's parking place. "That's Bob," she said. "I wonder why he's here tonight. I told him we were going." A frown knitted her creamy brow. "Do you mind waiting a moment? I should talk to him."

"Go ahead." Lance glanced at Bob, the burly biker who'd worn leather and chains at the Wild Moose. Tonight he was dressed in a clean black suit, with a red tie. His long curly hair had been wet and wrestled into a neat ponytail. In his hands was a bouquet of flowers.

Marissa moved toward him in her beautiful cocktail dress, her dark hair shining around her luminescent face, and Lance saw that she was desperately in love. That both of them were. She halted in front of him, and Bob thrust the flowers at her, obviously not entirely comfortable with the gesture. Marissa, in her open way, bent her head to the flowers and breathed deeply.

In ten seconds, Lance knew he wasn't taking Marissa to the dance. Sure enough, she talked for a while, then came back to the car. Bob headed inside.

She got in and sat down. "Bob wants to take me to the dance at the country club. He really didn't want to, which is why I asked you, but I think—" a dazzled, pleased expression crossed her face "—he really likes me."

"Don't sound so surprised! You're a hell of a woman. Go ahead and go."

"Are you sure you won't think I'm a cad?"

He chuckled. "I'm sure."

"I have a few minutes. Do you want to tell me what's bothering you?"

The sudden question, put so clearly, nearly made Lance choke up. "I'm just in love," he admitted. "Nothing a little time won't cure."

"With Tamara?"

"Yeah." He clenched his jaw tight to keep his emotions from rising out and spilling into his throat. "Yeah, she's the one."

Marissa cocked her head. "So, what's the problem? I don't get it. You're in love with her, she's in love with you—this is a problem?"

"I'm not that kind of man."

"What kind?"

"Reliable. Decent. All those warm fuzzy things a woman like her needs."

Marissa laughed. "You've been listening to your own reputation for way too long, Mr. Forrest. You might have been a bad boy a long time ago, but all I've seen in you is a rock-solid steadiness. You're aching to take care of her, to have a family and settle down." She grinned. "Just do it."

"What if I end up like my father? What if I let her down?"

"Your mother will kick your butt."

For the first time in a week, he actually smiled. And nodded. "I won't keep you, honey. Go on and get your guy."

She nodded, then leaned forward and put her hand on his arm. "Just one thing, Lance. I want you to think about what it would be like for you if you don't take this chance, and someone else comes along for Tamara. I want you to imagine her married to someone else." She kissed his cheek this time. "Think about it, okay?"

"I will. Have a good time. Call me and tell me how it goes with that certain snotty blonde, will you?"

She laughed. "Oh, I will." She paused, her hand on the door. "Remember, sweetie, the ones who never fall always fall hardest when they do."

The words echoed in him as he drove home then changed out of his good suit into a pair of reliable comfortable jeans. In his still-faceless apartment, he heated a TV dinner and watched an idiotic movie, feeling restless and lonely and—lost.

It was the same feeling that had been dogging him for his last three years in Houston. He liked the city, liked his company, liked his friends, but the hollowness never left him. And the weird thing was, he'd had no earthly idea what was bothering him until the telegram about his father had come. He was homesick.

But he was home now, so what was the problem? It felt like homesickness again.

I want you to imagine her married to someone else.

Marissa's words hit him hard. And he forced himself to do exactly that—imagine Tamara married to another man. Cooking for him. Laughing with him. Making love to him.

The lost, restless feeling in his chest rose to a keening howl. He nearly choked on it.

And suddenly, he knew that it was homesickness he felt. He was pining for the home he wanted to build, pining for the woman he wanted to share it with. He was pining for his family—the family that existed, and the one he hoped to build.

In relief, he bowed his head, and for the first time, in twenty years, he wept. Wept the long-halted tears of grief for his father, for the man he could have been and the man he had been, for the lost years his mother had spent on her children, even for Valerie.

It wasn't manly. It wasn't macho. His brothers would snicker for days if they knew. It didn't even last long because he ended up feeling completely stupid.

But it helped. When he raised his head, his heart was clear and full of purpose. The lostness was gone.

He knew what he had to do.

Tamara drove to Denver Saturday, to arrange her classes for the following semester. Her excitement over the trip got her through the awkward moments at Louise Forrest's house, those moments when Tamara looked around eagerly for signs of Lance and found none. After the last incident at her house, they'd agreed it would be better if they didn't see each other in person for a while, and worked out this arrangement with Louise.

It didn't really help much. Tamara missed him desperately. She ignored it as much as possible, but it seemed there was always a little voice in her heart crying his name. All the time, day and night.

But this morning, she shoved him out of her mind. Not even a broken heart would spoil her joy at finally returning to school, to the classes she loved and that would lead to the life she had missed so desperately. If she couldn't have Lance, at least she'd have this.

Walking around the Denver campus, Tamara found herself looking at it all with a different eye. The taste of intellectual energy and infinite possibility lingered in the crisp late-autumn air, and the smell of challenge filled her head, but it wasn't quite as heady as it once had been. She didn't have quite the same need to become absorbed into the university itself, to be a molecule within its vast, hallowed structure. As much as she looked forward to her classes, they would be a means to an end this time.

She mused at the change on her way home. What had the university represented to her as a young girl that she'd found elsewhere?

Identity. Yes, that was it. She'd been so afraid that she would disappear if she didn't affiliate herself with the university life. That somehow life would snatch her back into its bowels if she didn't keep her hands on those walls.

Cody had changed that for her. Cody—and Lance—who had each given her, in different ways, the courage to be herself, to claim her own life, within or without a structure.

What freedom!

A note was pinned to her door when she got home. It looked like Lance's handwriting, and Tamara felt an immediate sense of worry. She tore open the envelope and found a note in a childish scrawl. "Look in the bread box."

She smiled. A treasure hunt. What fun.

In the bread box, she found another note. In Lance's handwriting was a line of a poem. "'And all that's best of dark and bright / Meet in her aspect and her eyes.'"

Tamara swallowed. Byron.

The note directed her to go to the drugstore and ask the clerk for the next note. Feeling silly and a quiet anticipation, Tamara drove there. The older woman behind the counter smiled broadly. "Oh, yes." She gave her an envelope, her eyes twinkling. Tamara carried it outside before she opened it.

The quotation this time was from Ben Jonson. "'The thirst that from the soul doth rise/Doth ask a drink divine.'" Below it was a child's handwriting: "Go to the Wild Moose."

Her hands started to tremble, and Tamara had to take several long deep breaths before she pulled her car out and headed to the Wild Moose, where the waitress gave her another card. There was a secret in her eyes, and Tamara's heart began to thud painfully. This one contained another part of the Ben Jonson poem, "To Celia." Tamara knew it by heart. "'Drink to me only with thine eyes, and I will pledge with mine,'" he'd written.

Tamara finished it under her breath: "'Or leave a kiss but in the cup/ And I'll not look for wine.'" With effort, she bit back a rush of tears.

The chase led all over town, to the gas station, the courthouse, the school. By the time Tamara got the last note, telling her to go to Lake Rosalie, her heart was shimmering, and her hands trembled violently and she didn't think she could bear to have the suspense drawn out another second.

There seemed to be no one about. Tamara drove up and turned off her car. It was utterly still and peaceful when she got out. A magpie called out boldly, and she heard the twitterings of sparrows hidden by the pines. In the late-afternoon sunlight, the lake sparkled. Only her heart, pounding like a drum, seemed to break the quiet.

A picnic table sat by the lake, and on it was a simple flag made of paper and glitter, with her name in a childish scrawl. Below it was a card and a small package. She looked around, but there was no one.

She picked up the card. It was hand folded, and she recognized Cody's crayon style in the design on the front. For a moment, she thought of Lance patiently helping him as they put together the treasure hunt, and her chest hurt.

There was only a quotation this time. Shakespeare, from *Hamlet*. This time, Tamara could not breathe, and she could not stop the overflow of tears that spilled out of her eyes, hot and silent, as she read it aloud.

"Doubt thou the stars are fire;
Doubt that the sun doth move;
Doubt truth to be a liar
But never doubt I love."

Blinking, she picked up the wrapped package, unable to see for a moment. It was wrapped simply in white tissue paper, and on the top, written in blue ballpoint pen, was a single word—" 'Please.' "

She opened the box. Inside were three rings—a simple, stunning diamond that gave off hot sparks in the low sunlight, and two gold bands. Her hands were trembling so violently, Tamara could barely hold the small box.

From the trees came a rustling. Lance, holding Cody on his hip, emerged from the bushes. Man and boy had leaves in their hair, and the knees of their jeans had dirt marks from kneeling.

Lance said nothing. On his face was a sober, earnest expression, and Tamara had never been so in love with him as she was in that minute. She burst into tears.

He came forward and gently set Cody down on the ground. Tamara flung her arms around Lance's neck and wept with pure, unbridled joy. He caught her close, his arms like a vise around her body. She buried her face in his shoulder, smelling in his precious scent. "I can't imagine anything more touching. Not if I live a thousand years."

"I meant every word," he said in a husky voice. "I know I haven't had the best reputation, but I can't stand to think of my life without you, Tamara. I love you so much."

She clung to him, almost dizzy with joy. She thought of his faithfulness to his son, of his need to care for them, of his patience and honor and goodness. "You are such a good man," she whispered.

"Is that a yes?" he asked, and to her surprise, there was genuine doubt in his words.

She raised her head. "Yes."

He sighed, and the sound was replete with relief. He hugged her again, so close Tamara felt he would inhale her. "Thank God."

"And Valerie," Tamara said.

Lance smiled. "And Valerie," he agreed.

"Mommy," Cody piped up suddenly. "Don't you want to put on this pretty ring?"

Tamara laughed. "Oh, yes," she said, and held out her hand.

Cody looked hopefully at his father. "Can I do it?"

"Let's do it together." He took the ring out of the box and held it in his hand. Cody jumped on the picnic table to put his fingers over his dad's. Together they slid the ring onto Tamara's finger. She admired it happily, then hugged them both at once. "You guys are terrific," she said.

"That's because of you, Mommy," Cody replied seriously.

"Amen," said Lance.

In the forest clearing, with her son and her future mate in her arms, Tamara felt her soul fly up and touch the sky, mingle with the waters of the lake, dance on the wind.

"I love you, Lance," she breathed. All was well.

He pressed a kiss to her brow. "And I love you, Tamara."

"And me!" Cody shouted.

Tamara and Lance laughed. "And you, too," they said together.

*   *   *   *   *

In July 1997,
Book 2 of THE LAST ROUNDUP *moves to*
Intimate Moments with RECKLESS *(IM #796).*
Jake Forrest, the oldest of the Forrest brothers,
was once a high-ranking military officer.
Now he has come home to Red Creek, Colorado—
trying to escape the demons of his warrior past.
But the only place he can find peace is in the arms
of the most unlikely woman in town....

This summer, the legend
continues in Jacobsville

A LONG, TALL
TEXAN SUMMER

Three **BRAND-NEW** short stories

This summer, Silhouette brings readers a special
collection for Diana Palmer's LONG, TALL TEXANS
fans. Diana has rounded up three **BRAND-NEW**
stories of love Texas-style, all set in Jacobsville,
Texas. Featuring the men you've grown to love from
this wonderful town, this collection is a must-have
for all fans!

*They grow 'em tall in the saddle in Texas—and
they've got love and marriage on their minds!*

Don't miss this collection of original Long, Tall Texans
stories...available in June at your favorite retail outlet.

▼ *Silhouette*®
™

LTTST

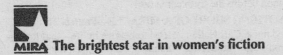

From the bestselling author of
Iron Lace and *Rising Tides*

EMILIE RICHARDS

JANET DAILEY
AWARD
WINNER

**When had the love and promises they'd shared turned
into conversations they couldn't face, feelings they
couldn't accept?**

Samantha doesn't know how to fight the demons that
have come between her and her husband, Joe. But she
does know how to fight for something she wants: a child.

But the trouble is Joe. Can he accept that he'll never be the
man he's expected to be—and can he seize this one chance
at happiness that may never come again?

THE TROUBLE WITH JOE

"A great read and a winner in every sense of the word!"
—Janet Dailey

Available in June 1997
at your favorite retail outlet.

MIRA The brightest star in women's fiction

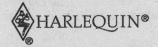

And the Winner Is...
You!

...when you pick up these great titles
from our new promotion at your
favorite retail outlet this June!

Diana Palmer
The Case of the Mesmerizing Boss

Betty Neels
The Convenient Wife

Annette Broadrick
Irresistible

Emma Darcy
A Wedding to Remember

Rachel Lee
Lost Warriors

Marie Ferrarella
Father Goose

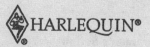